C

Th

Lee Kenny was born in London and raised in Walsall, in the West Midlands. After getting a job as a Trainee Reporter on the Sutton Coldfield Observer he has worked as a journalist in Birmingham, New Zealand and China. He currently teaches journalism at University of Kent, writes about documentary film and goes to the cinema as often as he can.

The Betamax Theory is his debut novel.

The Betamax Theory

Lee Kenny

Green Door Books

GREEN DOOR BOOKS

Published by Green Door Books

Green Door Books, London, England

First published in 2014
Copyright © Lee Kenny 2014
All right reserved

Edited by A. Ingram

Set in 11/13 Garamond
Typeset by Green Door Books, London.

Cover design M. Reynolds/L.Kenny

ISBN-10:
1500791326

Note

This book would not have been possible without the support of a number of people. I would like to thank Abi Ingram for her dedication to editing the manuscript and for her inspired help in developing the story. Iain Grant for his kind words and advice after reading the first draft many years ago. Laura Mander, Vikki Quartermain and John Newton for their continued help and encouragement. Matt Reynolds, Mark Hobson and Aidan Byrne for helping me complete the mission.

Lastly, thanks to Robert Zemeckis and Bob Gale for making time travel seem possible.

To my beloved Sarah, who I've enjoyed travelling through time with.

And to Kev, John & John for making me a film fan.

Prologue

Monday May 6th 1985

My Uncle Robert died on a Sunday morning and my Dad got
the news from one of his cousins the following day. It was
hard to know how to act. I remember feeling sad for my
Dad but I desperately wanted to go to Kev Robinson's
house to play on his new radio controlled car, a high-speed
off-road racer called The Hornet. We'd spent months
standing outside the window of J. Slater Electricals,
memorising the specifications of the 1/10 scale, two-wheel
drive dirt buggy with its independent swing-axle suspension
and front friction dampers, and now - after pooling all of his
birthday and paper round money - he'd got one. But we
weren't allowed out that day. My Mom said it would be
disrespectful and that we should be there for my Dad, so
while I tried to memorise a deck of Top Trumps and Dave
flicked though the catalogue looking at watches, Linda
moaned about not being able to go to the cinema with her
friends. As it was, my Dad seemed fine and the only real
difference that day was that Mom said we should say a prayer
for Uncle Robert before we started our Sunday dinner. We
closed our eyes, tilted our heads and I wondered whether
Kev would be racing The Hornet over the woods or whether
he'd decided to stick to his quiet cul-de-sac until he'd got the
measure of its Mabuchi 540 motor.

1

My Mom, Dad and Linda went up for the funeral the following week, while Dave and I went to our Nan's. The day, they said, went well and other than the occasional mention, Uncle Robert faded quickly from conversation and eventually, it seemed, from our collective memory. That is until the letter arrived. With no children and no next of kin, Uncle Robert's estate was to be split between my Dad and his five cousins, and his solicitor said the beneficiaries were to attend a meeting in a fortnight's time to hear how his things were to be divided up.

"Are we gonna be rich?" Dave asked excitedly when Mom explained why Dad would be making another trip to Nottingham.

"Yeah," Linda chipped in, "Charlotte Randal's Nan died last year and they got enough to go on a cruise, and buy a new car."

I sat at the kitchen table eating a banana sandwich, listening in.

"Well Uncle Robert wasn't well off. And anyway I don't like you talking like that," Mom replied sharply. "He was elderly and he didn't have a lot. It'll mostly be sentimental things, I imagine."

"What about his house? That must be worth a bit," Linda asked, all too aware of the property boom we were in.

"It's a council house and don't be so….," my Mom struggled to find the right word.

"Mercenary," called my Dad from his armchair in the living room, settling the discussion.

As it turned out, as well as some Edwardian furniture and a

2

sizeable Royal Doulton crockery collection that belonged to his Mom, Uncle Robert had a Post Office account that at the time of his death contained £6,523.46. As well as the six nephews and nieces the sum was to be shared by the Nottingham All Services Club, meaning a cheque was made to my Dad for £931.92. The cousins and Stan, the treasurer of the All Services Club, decided that the remaining items were to be sold-off and a memorial bench would be installed at Beacon Street Bowling Club where Uncle Robert and Stan would often visit for lunch and a pint.

The following week, I got home from school late as I'd stayed behind for Chess Club. My Dad's car was already on the drive and I noticed a sense of excitement as I entered the front door and hung my coat in the hall.

"Mart, come in here", Linda called from the living room.

I slid my school shoes off and could hear laughter and loud voices.

"Nearly. Nearly," said Dave. "Back a bit, you've nearly got it".

Pushing the door open I saw all four of them sitting around the television, my Dad and Dave on the floor, my Mom and Linda on the settee.

"Dad's brought a video recorder," Linda explained excitedly as I stepped into the room. "It's got a remote control and everything".

I looked over at the television cabinet in disbelief; hardly anyone in my class had a video recorder.

"It's just like Uncle Peter's, he got it from Dixons today, didn't you Dad?"

My Dad murmured a response as he fiddled behind the telly.
"Back a bit, back a bit," guided Dave as a faint outline of the
Six o'clock News emerged from the fizzing static.
"There. Hold it there," Dave called as a serious looking man
standing outside a hospital appeared on the screen.
"What do you think?" Mom asked.
"I dunno," I replied, too shocked to think. "Can I get
Grange Hill on it?"
"Course you can," Linda scoffed.
"And films?"
"Whatever you want. I'm going to tape EastEnders and keep
them in my room, aren't I Mom? And we can go to the
video shop and hire videos".
"We'll see," Mom replied, "We're not having any of those
Video Nasties in here".
I genuinely couldn't believe it. I'd watched videos at my
cousin Danny's but never imagined we would have one, it
seemed too extravagant in a household where we shared the
bathwater and it was inconceivable to go to McDonald's
unless it was your birthday.
"It's from the money off Uncle Robert, and we're getting
new bedroom suites and Mom and Dad are going on a
second honeymoon next year," Linda continued with a
squeal of excitement, but I'd tuned-out. All I could think
about were the possibilities that opened up. Dave and Dad
continued to scroll through the channels and the Allied
Carpets' logo appeared advertising their Price Breaker Sale
before fading into a noise of grey and black pixels. My Mom
leaned forward on the settee, peering over her glasses

4

expectantly. I looked down at the brown cardboard box it had arrived in; an owner's manual lay open but unread on the brown and red rug by the fireplace. It was a Betamax Sanyo Betacord Video Cassette Recorder, a silver and black case with seven buttons in the middle and a pop-up slot to load the videos into - it was the most futuristic thing I'd ever seen.

With all four channels tuned-in my Dad set the digital clock and sat back to survey his work.

"So, what'd you think?" he asked, slightly out of breath. Linda did a little clap, Dave nodded approvingly and I simply stared at him with delight.

"Let's give it a go," my Mom suggested and handed my Dad the remote control as we ducked the three metres of thin black cord that connected it to the video.

"Well then, what do you wanna record?" he asked as he flicked through the night's telly from the comfort of his armchair.

As the months and years went by, my life became inextricably linked to that silver and black machine in the corner of the room. I spent hours scouring the Radio Times for programmes to record, shows that dictated the friendships I would form and the daydreams I would have as I whiled away my maths lessons. I watched the James Bond films my Nan had seen at the cinema and horror movies Dave and his friends knew I was too young for. I fell in love with Princess Leia and marvelled as Indiana Jones dangled from the front of a Nazi truck. I taped the first episode of Knight Rider (Knight of the Juggernaut) and more than 80 episodes of The A Team. I memorised the plots and dialogue of The Goonies, Inner Space and Crocodile Dundee and rented every film the British Board of Film Classification and the bloke at the video shop would allow me to see.

When Betamax finally lost out to the better marketed VHS system, Uncle Peter took my Mom into town to replace it. As the only child left at home it was relocated to my room, where I'd tape episodes of The Word, Twin Peaks and The Fresh Prince of Bel-Air, as well as Betty Blue and Last Tango in Paris, when they were screened during a late-night 'European Season'. When it was consigned to the loft in the late-90s I was head-over-heels in love with films. Betamax may have become a byword for the also-ran, the plucky Japanese underdog that didn't know when to quit, but I couldn't have wished for a better companion during my teenage years. We never got our new bedroom suites and Mom and Dad never got their honeymoon but my Uncle Robert gave me a more lasting legacy, a place to escape to.

Chapter One

Monday November 7th 2005

My alarm clock sounded early that morning and I pressed snooze to buy myself an extra nine minutes. I'd been up until late watching Jaws 2 the night before and fell asleep on the settee just as Mike and Sean Brody defied their Dad's warning and embarked on their ill-advised sailing trip. I must have muted the television at some point because when I woke just after half three, a repeat of that week's Panorama beamed silently out from the corner of the room. I was cold and huddled under my jacket that I'd thrown down the side of the armchair when I got home from the chip shop on Friday night. I had a stiff neck from laying on my side and cramp in my up-stretched legs. Shuffling to bed I was annoyed and told myself to stop watching DVDs on a Sunday night. The alarm sounded and I reached across and snoozed-it again. Lying under the heavy winter quilt my eyes fell closed and I drifted into a strange half-sleep, both dreaming and thinking about the day ahead. The alarm sounded for a third time and I calculated my routine.

"Get up, get dressed, wolf down two pieces of toast, brush my teeth, do my hair, apply some body spray and race to the station."

"Twenty minutes ought to do it," I thought and pressed snooze again.

Drifting into another warm, dreamy state I thought about my day. It should be fairly quiet. Check last night's tills, order-in some new cleaning products, speak to Dennis, finalise next month's rotas, unload the new deliveries. "Shit. The deliveries," I blurted out as I bolted out of bed. In the two years I'd been supervisor the stock deliveries had always been on a Tuesday, giving me and whoever else was on a fairly cushy start to the week. But Head Office had changed the delivery days meaning mine would now be between 8.30 and 9.30 on Monday mornings. Scrabbling around the floor I found two black socks and threw on Friday's trousers. I grabbed a clean shirt from the wardrobe and searched for my shoes, trying to remember where I'd kicked them off as I'd poured red sauce over a battered sausage and chips. My regulation uniform was black trousers, a white shirt, a company-issued black and yellow tie, a white knee-length overcoat and a white hygienic Trilby. My hat was in my locker at work but two of my three overcoats were wet in the washing machine and the other one was on the back of the kitchen chair. I folded it quickly and stuffed it into my backpack, ran my fingers through my flattened hair and raced out of the door.

It was a ten minute walk or a five minute jog to the station. It was just under a mile but I'd given up trying to run it without having to stop at least once. I caught my breath and with my feet slapping on the pavement, I sprinted along Osborne Road, feeling both sick from running and hungry due to the lack of breakfast.

8

I cursed the inventor of the alarm clock snooze button as I turned right and waited for a gap in the traffic. I crossed Station Road and used the last of my strength to power myself up the slope to the platform.

"This is a customer announcement; the 7.42 service to Birmingham New Street is delayed by approximately nine minutes."

Standing there I wiped the sweat off my forehead and tried to disguise my heavy breathing. My lungs and throat burned and my arms tingled with cold and adrenaline. When the train arrived I took my seat, closed my eyes for a minute and told myself I needed to start jogging.

I looked out of the window and wondered what the week would bring.

"At least I made it", I thought, "At least I will be there to meet the deliveries."

I looked around the rest of the carriage, it was full with fellow commuters heading for the City.

I always like the sound of that, that I worked for a large company in the City, even if the city was Birmingham, and most people called it 'Town' anyway.

"Yeah I work in the City," I remember telling a girl at Paul's 30th. She looked at me like I was the stupid one.

"Oh? Up Town?" she said.

At a time when other places were vying for city status, it seemed like the people of Birmingham wanted their city to be relegated back to a town.

"I wonder what the Arch Bishop would think if we told him he has to sell-off the cathedral," I joked in reply, but I'd already lost her by that stage and she said she had to go and find her friends.

But I did work in the City and I loved the fact that when I boarded the train of a morning with the other commuters we were indistinguishable from one another. For 13 minutes I could have been the young hot-shot at a top law firm or the recently promoted junior partner at one of the big old financial institutions, or have founded my own marketing company from scratch, like Rob's brother-in-law from Solihull.

As the train left Erdington and I reached into my bag for a book or the paper I was in the club with every other young executive on our way to the office.

My phone rang that morning as we headed into Aston. Cradling my flash new handset so the camera lens was visible, I waited a second before answering.

"Hello, Martin speaking," I said, sounding sharp, professional.

"Mart, it's me." It was Linda.

"Hi, how are things?" The bloke next to me glanced my way.

"Fine. Are you still coming over tonight to do Dad's grave?" She asked. It was more of a demand than a request.

"Yep, yep. Course I am. Yep, that's fine." Was that too many 'yeps'?

"What time?"

"I can be away by five thirty and at yours for seven." Damn, I clearly wasn't talking business anymore. But it could be drinks after work.

"Aw Mart," she whined. "Can't you get here any earlier? It'll be too late by then." She was one of the few people who still called me Mart.

"I'll check my diary when I get in and see if I can move things around."

Unless I'm mistaken, I thought, that's twice now the girl opposite has looked up from her book.

"Well, I need to be back by half seven to do Craig's tea and get the girls to bed."

I caught myself biting my fingernails and put my right hand down by my side. I looked out of the window, then back to the girl opposite and wondered where she worked. She was in her mid-twenties, no ring and looked a bit like Sienna Miller. She was reading Jonathon Coe. I wondered what she was called. Probably not something exotic like Sienna. More girl-next doorish; Sarah, Abigail or maybe Katherine. As I watched, I willed her to look up again. Go on Katherine, look up.

"That's fine I'll be there earlier," I told Linda. "Should I bring anything?" Excellent. Sounded like I was going to a dinner party. Go on Katherine, look up.

"You said you were gonna borrow Paul's strimmer. You haven't forgotten have you? You've had all weekend." Katherine had a black handbag and a carrier from H&M. She looked down intently at her book, The Rotters' Club.

"He was away at the weekend but I'll speak to him later." I really liked her boots. If she looks up again, should I smile, I wondered.

"You'd better not be trying to get out of this. I'm not having Mom seeing it in a state again." Probably not, a smile could look sleazy. Maybe just look coy in a 'how embarrassing to be arranging this on the train' sort of way.

"No, honestly it's going to be fine. Just difficult to talk, I'm on the train." Look up Katherine, I implored. In the seat behind me a phone rang.

"Hello, Andrew speaking. Ian, good morning." It sounded important, and a bit pompous.

Linda chirped in again: "So can you get to mine for six?" There were sounds of traffic and crying in the background, she must have been driving the kids to school.

"I'll see if I can get an early finish. I'm gonna be in meetings most of the morning but I'll call you at lunch." Brilliant. The bit about meetings sounded really good. But was lunch still for wimps? Naw, we're supposed to be eating five-a-day these days. There was that thing in GQ about how a healthy lifestyle was the third highest priority for today's young professionals.

Linda was getting harassed: "What?" I was annoying her now. "Oh, Mart just phone me later."

"Ok, I'll-"

"But I'll have my phone off at the hospital. Have you been to see Nan yet?" I knew she was going to ask that.

"No, not yet. No time really. I'll arrange something this week." I looked back across. Oh, go on Katherine, look up.

"I've told you the times. Ten 'til two and five 'til eight, but she starts the chemo on Wednesday so you can't see her then and Auntie Cath will be...... Hang on." The phone went silent, that was my chance.

"Yep, that's fine; I'll tell Claire to put something in the diary

12

and see if I can arrange an earlier flight." Excellent. That was excellent. But shit, should I have told Claire or asked her? No, she's my imaginary secretary; I think I can tell her. Surely *that* would make her look up. The phone came back on.

"Look, I've got to go. And Mart please don't be late." Again, more of an order than a request. I was just about to reply when she started screaming. The same scream she used when we were kids, only now she used it to shout at her kids. "I've bloody told you two," she shrieked, her voice getting higher with each word. Then one of the kids wailed. Linda threatened to kill the pair of them and the other one shouted how it wasn't her fault. I'm fairly sure that if the train had been moving, or if people had been boarding, or if I'd had the volume down a bit it might have been ok. Linda's threats and my nieces' protests might have been lost to the sound of the engine or the hubbub of alighting passengers. But she could be so loud, and as we sat motionless, ready to pull into New Street Station, everybody heard. They heard that my nieces were going to bed without any tea that night, and how Michelle wasn't going to Catherine's house on Friday. They heard the screaming, the arguing and whose fault it was and how it wasn't fair, and how Linda was sick of me lately and how she wasn't doing Dad's grave on her own again like last year. Don't look up.

"I'm telling ya Mart, Mom's got too much on her plate without you acting up again."

"I know," I mumbled.

"And I want this to be special, Mom does too. You know it's

13

the anniversary?" Of course it's the anniversary; it's the anniversary every bloody year. Please don't look up. My gaze was fixed firmly on the floor.

"I'll be there at six. See you later."

"Bye."

I hung-up and slid my phone back into my jacket pocket. I crumpled down into my seat and watched the rain streaming down the dirty window as the train sat waiting for a green light. We'd been there 30 seconds before a phone rang opposite me and I discreetly glanced over as Katherine reached down into the smart black bag sat between her matching black boots. As she leant forward I caught a glimpse of her bra, it was white.

"Hello," she said, sounding lovely.

"Morning babe. No. I'm still on the train, can I call you back in a bit?" Of course she had a boyfriend; I don't even know why I was surprised.

"Ok, I'll pop in on my way to court," she said before whispering goodbye. I wish she hadn't looked over but as she closed her phone she glanced across. Without thinking I raised my eyebrows and she quickly looked down at her bag. The train pulled in and after patting down the pockets of my coat and trousers twice, I found my travel pass but as I reached the gate there was no one there to inspect tickets and a stream of people filtered through the narrow gap and over to the escalators.

It took about 10 minutes to reach work from the station and as I left the bulk of the commuters heading to their desks and computers I quickened my pace to try and beat the worst of the rain. I took out my name badge as I crossed the car park and pinned it to my shirt. It said Thompson's in proud yellow letters and below it read my name and position: Martin Brownlow, Area Supervisor.

Stepping through the main doors by the cigarette kiosk, I wondered if Debbie would be in this morning and what state the kitchens had been left in by the evening roster. I wondered how busy it would be and hoped I wouldn't get put on tills again like last Monday. On the way to my locker I knocked on Dennis' office door in the hope of catching him to finally book some of the time-off I was owed. His secretary Susan told me in her usual smug way that he was in meetings for most of the morning and that I'd have to leave him a message on his voicemail.

The aisles were already beginning to fill by the time I got to my department but we never got busy until lunchtime, there's little call for a roast chicken at nine in the morning. Checking my diary, I had thirty-five boxes of wings, breasts, thighs and nuggets to find a space for in the freezer and a note left for me said that Christine had phoned in sick again and that Rich Thomas had been moved onto Produce for the morning. Carl, the supervisor on Produce, came over and we talked about the weekend. He went out drinking on Broad Street and we were having a good chat about his mate getting pissed when he suddenly drew attention to a fat stain on the bottom of my white overcoat.

"Customers won't like that," he said. Bloody cheek, I thought, he was only the same level as me and I'd been there longer.

15

"And it's a bad example to the rest of the OC" he said as he turned and headed out the back. Carl talked in initials; lots of people did since Dennis arrived. Dennis was the boss, the store manager, a man so urgently in demand that he didn't have time to talk in proper words. He abbreviated everything and because he did, a lot of other people did too. The OC was the Oven Counter, my department. The CDs were the Cash Desks or checkouts to the customers. CAB stood for Cakes and Bakery and the WAS was Wine and Spirits. The HEA was the home entertainment aisle and even the books got shortened to HBs and PBs. The stupidest of all was the DC, the deli-counter, which is already an abbreviation of delicatessen. I jovially mentioned that at one of the quarterly meetings and Dennis pulled me aside afterwards to tell me that he wouldn't be undermined by one of his juniors. It should have been different between Dennis and I. Despite usually being very cagey about his life outside of Thompson's he once let slip at an annual awards dinner that he went to Sutton Comp, my old school. Thinking I'd gauged it just right, I approached him afterwards as he was doing the rounds, displaying his 'Most Inspirational Leader 1998' trophy to a table of fawning middle managers.

"You grew up in Sutton?" I asked.

"What?" His wide eyes narrowing to a scowl.

"You said on stage you went to Sutton Comp, that was my old school," I continued to beam, finally glad of some common ground between us.

"I don't think that's any of your business Martin, do you?" he replied, heading-off to shake hands with Glenn Burrows

16

from the Bolton branch.

The next time I messed-up in front of him was when I called him DJ like the other managers did. He told me to call him Mr Johnson. Dennis was brought in to replace Ian Baxter who was pensioned-off early when the new extension opened a year earlier. He had been a miles better boss. You could have a laugh with him and talk about the football and wind him up when Scotland got beaten. He never used to mind it. Once, after a pile-up on the M6, loads of the deliveries were late getting through. When they finally arrived everyone not on tills was called out the back to get the goods unloaded. Ian organised a human chain from the delivery yard to the Warehouse and we emptied three lorries in no time. It was a classic day; people talked about it for years afterwards. There was a real Blitz spirit, everyone helping out; and at the front of the line, with his tie off and his sleeves rolled-up, was Ian. He was the old type of manager, not afraid to get his hands dirty and everyone respected him for it.

I caught up with Carl out the back.

"Have you seen Dennis this morning?" I asked.

"Yeah."

"What kind of mood's he in?"

"Alright. Why?"

"Oh, my Nan's in hospital, she's got cancer. I was hoping to finish a bit early today to go and see her. The visiting hours are really short and-"

"You'll be lucky." He actually smirked. Had he heard what I'd just said?

"Do you think? Why? Didn't Dennis' wife have cancer or something?"

"She had cysts, but ask him about it if you want to get sacked. He heard Sonia Allen talking about it and he gave her a verbal warning. That's why he moved her to Produce." Produce was still called Produce. Conversation over, Carl left to talk to Barry in WD, Warehouse and Deliveries. Barry was one of the last of the die-hards though and still called it the Warehouse. He and Mark were among the few people I counted as genuine allies after the restructuring. I watched Carl disappear behind the Salad Station then looked back to the counter. On the shelf behind the main oven I noticed a greasy pair of serving tongs, left there from the night before. I thought about writing a note in the diary to speak to the evening shift but decided against it. I took the tongs back into the kitchen, washed them up and placed them on the draining board. I stood there for a moment in the silence before heading back out the front to serve a lady two pieces of pork belly.

Chapter Two

My Dad died when I was 13 and to tell the truth I didn't remember much about him. And even then I was never sure if the memories I had were genuine or whether they had been pieced together from photos and stories told to me by my Mom. He worked as an insurance broker, was a heavy smoker and always read the local papers cover-to-cover. They are the three things I could say I knew about him for certain. Mom said he used to take me fishing when I was younger, and that I used to love the time that the two of us would spend together, but I don't really remember anything about those trips. His funeral was busy but not packed and I've always been told how many friends he had but never met any of them in the 20 years since he died. The day was a blur of sombre people I half recognised. I stood there in the church and back at our house nodding as people gathered around me saying how he'd gone to a better place. I remember thinking it was too bright a day for a funeral, the sun seemed to bleach everything white. Mom perched on the edge of the sofa clutching the same cup of tea as people came and went. Linda tried to sit beside her at one point, searching for comfort, but found none. I think that was the first time I realised we'd lost more than one parent in the crash. I don't really remember seeing Dave that day but he must have been somewhere. My Nan bustled around with plates of sandwiches, absent-mindedly patting me on the head as she walked past. She and Linda sat and cried after everyone had gone. Linda letting it all out as my Nan stroked her hair. My Mom's tears were the worst though. Once they started, they never seemed to stop. They were silent, slow tears at first, creeping from her eyes, pausing at the top of her cheeks like condensation gathering before teeming down a window. They'd continue to flow. They became as much a part of her face as the absent look in her eyes, the look that seemed to say there was no-one home, that she'd opted out. I sometimes used to wish that she would shout and wail her grief like I'd seen an African woman do on the telly. That seemed more natural somehow. If she shouted her pain, she could connect with it and begin to let go, making it possible for her to start to live again. But that never happened.

When I'd visit my Mom it would sometimes only take a few minutes before she'd produce a photo album and gesture for me to move from the armchair to the settee to sit and hear about a holiday we'd had or a wedding we'd been to, most of which I could hardly remember. I only really thought about my Dad when I was there flicking through the pages of history, looking at younger versions of us on the beach or in wedding clothes we'd ordered from the catalogue the month before. If my Dad was on my mind that week it was only because of the anniversary. My Mom wouldn't have it but he was a miserable sod and he was hardly ever there because he was working all the time. He used to go walking when I was much younger but for as long as I could remember his job and his hobby were the same thing: having a wife and three kids to look after. I think he was a good man. He never played away from home, never lost money at the bookies, never drank too much, but as far as I can tell, he led a dull life. He once smacked me really hard when I took Danny Godfrey down the shed to look at porno mags that we'd found, but I think it was more out of embarrassment than anger. He'd be 68, I thought, if he were still alive today. My Mom said the idea of doing a special service came to her in a dream and it was what he would have wanted. People always know what the dead would have wanted, especially my Mom. "Just make sure you do well in your exams, you know, for your Dad, it's what he would have wanted," she would coo in encouragement.

"Your Dad always wanted you to do A-Levels, you should stay on at Sixth Form", she advised.

"Oh, your Dad would be so proud if you went to University like he did." I wanted to take a year-off and go travelling around France but against my better judgement I went to Uni, like he would have wanted. I lasted three months before I jacked it in and was back home by the Christmas.

I started working nights at Thompson's until I got a proper job but after a while they offered me full-time hours and it was good money. Next year, I'll have been here for 15 years, I thought as I steered the pallet truck through toiletries and across into tinned goods.

"One and a half decades," I mumbled as I turned into the freezer section by the pizzas.

Over the PA an electric guitar version of Celine Dion's Think Twice lulled shoppers into a soporific-shuffle behind their trolleys and I turned into the Oven Counter where Steven stood waiting for me beside the walk-in refrigerator.

21

"I thought you were coming to help me," I asked.

"I was," he replied. He looked like he'd been smoking dope. He did that.

"I had to load 30 boxes on my own."

"Err, sorry," he shrugged. He wore a scruffy, bum-fluff moustache and his home-made tattoo was visible through the sleeve of his white shirt.

"Well, can you help me unload it then?" I asked.

My shirt and tie, white overall and hygienic trilby hat offered little protection from the cold blast of the freezer fan. We unloaded the boxes in silence. 15 years. Again I began to ponder. Why did it bother me so much? Five, ten, 12 years had come and gone without question but 15 had taken a hold of me. A sense of claustrophobia arose every time I thought about it. I think I was about nine or ten when my Uncle Peter sent me a birthday card with an illustrated picture of Kevin Keegan on the front. Inside he wrote: 'I look forward to the day we see you playing for England'. I used to think about that card a lot, especially at work and I hated him for writing it. As a kid I used to genuinely believe I would play for England and would drift-off to sleep imagining myself older, running onto the pitch at Wembley in the same white, V-necked t-shirt.

Steven huffed as he leant forward to shift the last of the crates. I broke the silence.

"How long have you been here for now, Steven?" I asked as he passed me a box of frozen birds.

"At Thompson's? Dunno. Two years?"

"Yeah?"

"Yeah. A year here and a year on fish."

"Oh. And why did you ask for the transfer?" I enquired.

"Don't like fish."

"Oh. But was that it? Was there anything else? You know, new job, new challenge, new people?"

"Naw, just hated the smell of fish."

We shifted more boxes and a few moments passed before I followed up with a more direct line of questioning.

"So how long do you think you'll work here for?" I asked, but Steven went on the defensive.

"Are you gonna give me a verbal warning or something?"

"No. Course not, I was just wondering."

"Oh. Well I've gotta work here. Just had a kid and me girlfriend's Mom won't let me see 'im unless I give 'er 50 quid a wick."

"Oh, ok." And I actually began to feel a little bit relieved. Two years here, a kid and a crap moustache. Probably still lives with his Mom.

"You got your own place?" I asked, knowing I shouldn't really pry.

"Naw, can't afford it. Still at home."

We finished up and Steven said he would take the pallet truck back to the Warehouse.

"Thanks," I said.

"Er. Alright if I have a quick fag on the way back?" he asked cautiously. Smoking was one of Dennis' pets hates.

"Go for it," I told him. Poor bloke, it was the least I could do.

I stood alone in the freezer for a moment and looked at the

23

piled-up boxes, they reminded me of Jim, my old supervisor. He was great, strict but fair. He caught Simon and I once out the back throwing knives into boxes from across the other side of the room. We'd been to see the Steven Segal film Under Siege the week before and we'd say his line ('I'm just a cook'), before dispatching the knives into our cardboard terrorists. Yes, we were breaking Health and Safety but Jim was fine about it because we'd done our work. We'd cleaned the oven and the counters and we were just killing time at the end of the night. You couldn't get away with that sort of thing now. The place had changed for the worst.

"Martin!" A voice snapped me out of my daydream.

"Yes. Just coming," I called, racing out of the freezer.

"What are you doing? Why is no one out front?" It was Dennis, his daily inspection was early.

"Yvonne should be here. I'll-"

"I've just seen her in LA with Laura Mackin." Lifestyles and Accessories. "Who else is on?"

"It's just me and Steven Barnes. Richard has gone to cover on Produce. I was just unloading-"

"So where's Steven?"

"WD."

"Well that's no excuse. Someone needs to be out here at all times. You know that, we've talked about it before."

"I know, I…."

"There were two women waiting. I asked them to come back in a moment. God knows how many other people have walked away assuming we were closed."

"The ovens are on so-"

"But if there's no one here to serve the customers, the customers are going to go elsewhere."

"You're right," I agreed, trying to placate him.

"Is that a stain on your overall?"

"Yes, it's...." I gave up, what was the point? "Sorry, I know. The customers won't like it."

"Yeah, I'm sorry too. You're a nice guy Martin, the customers seem to like you, the staff like you, most of the managers here like you, but you were not made a supervisor to be nice."

I nodded.

"Susan said you wanted to see me."

"Oh right, yeah. I just wondered if…"

Steven came back stinking of fags. Dennis clocked it immediately.

"Where have you been?" he demanded to know.

"Out the back of the Warehouse," he said, looking down at the floor. For God's sake, I thought, at least call it the WD.

"Doing what?" Dennis' face was beginning to go red. It did that.

"Just having a quick ciggie," he said before glancing at me. "Martin said it was ok."

I was basically screwed. Dennis looked at me in sheer disgust and then at his watch.

"I don't have time for this. Martin come and see me this afternoon at three thirty, I'll ask Carl to cover for you." He didn't wait for a reply, he turned and left.

"Did I......?" Steven asked as he finally twigged.

"No, it's ok. Just serve that woman would you".

He shrugged and headed over to the fried chicken counter, his lace untied on his left shoe.

There are regulars at supermarkets like everywhere else. And just like the locals at the Dog and Duck, they have particular orders. There were lots of familiar faces that I saw week-in, week-out, but there was a select group of favourites whose visits genuinely improved my day. Looking back I suppose my top three regulars would have been the sheepish pensioner, the really nice smelling prostitute and the red sauce man. I saw them almost every week for years; in the case of the pensioner it was twice a week, more than my own mother. She had no kids but instead doted-on her two dogs, an Alsatian and a Collie. She bought chicken from Thompson's for years and every time she'd used the same old line, delivered like it was the first.

"Have you got any broken ones?" She'd ask, gesturing towards the roast chickens. "For me dogs."

According to company policy I should have told her that we weren't able to serve the broken ones and pointed her to the pet food aisle, but I didn't, I found a bird with a slightly detached wing, popped it in a bag and charged her half price for it. I know Dennis would have looked at it differently but I saw it as good customer service. She came in every Monday and Thursday for a half-price chicken and left with a basket of shopping. After a while it'd reached the stage where I deliberately sabotaged the biggest chicken on display at about 6.30pm so she could ask with a clear conscience. Whether they were for her dogs or whether she lived off those chickens I'll never know but the look of gratitude she gave me was worth every penny of the £1.44 she saved at Thompson's twice a week.

The really nice smelling prostitute came in on Sunday afternoons. I had no confirmation of her profession other than Claire Dawson said her brother knew her and that 'she was a pro'. She was gorgeous, with long dark hair, pillar box red lips and among the rare few who wore high heels and a short skirt to do her weekly shopping. She sometimes came in with a bloke, who Claire reckoned was her pimp but I said I didn't think they would necessarily do their shopping together. He was a thick-set, Phil Mitchell-type and looked like he'd probably done time, but then again he could have been a plumber or a fighter pilot for all we knew. Either way, her visits were always widely anticipated by the Sunday staff who, despite it being our busiest period of the week, always found time to drool lustfully or to slag-off her clothes and make up. She always smelt lovely too - to cover up the smell of blokes' cum, it'd been suggested - but in a desert of chicken fat and oven cleaner she was an oasis of strawberries and hairspray. The red sauce man liked nothing more than a quarter bottle of ketchup poured over his chicken breasts. I once chatted to him about how cars were getting smaller and he went and told Dennis how courteous I'd been.

With such familiarity with my customers, who also included Mr Bevan and his 'deaf aid', the post-match footballers from the 'Rec' and the drunken postman, I was almost speechless that morning when Rachel Dixon approached the counter. "Do I need to take a number?" she asked.

27

I recognised her instantly. I also noticed she wasn't wearing a wedding ring but that she had two multi-packs of yogurts in her basket; only Moms buy that many yogurts, I thought.

"Er, no, we did away with that," I replied. She clearly didn't recognise me and I couldn't think if that was a good or a bad thing.

"Oh?"

She looked incredible. The last I'd heard she was living in London.

"Yeah, we did a customer survey in 2003 and the majority of shoppers said it made them feel like the wait was longer. You know? Staring at the screen, looking at your ticket, waiting for your number to come up, wondering how long it's going to take and thinking should I carry on shopping and pop back in a bit or should I hang on and wait?" I couldn't believe it was her. She was the best looking girl in school and once, 20 years ago, she almost kissed me. "From personal experience, I'd actually say it was a faster system but, you know, 'the customer's always right', right?" That sounded stupid.

She smiled politely before there was a moment of recognition: "Didn't you go to Sutton Comp?"

"Yeah," I nodded.

"You're Martin Brownlow. You got mugged."

"Yes, I did. Rachel isn't it? Rachel Dixon?"

"It was. It's Rachel Watson now." She's married, damn.

"You're married, cool."

"Was married, I just never changed it back."

"Ok. So are you still acting? Didn't you go down to

London?"

"Oh, a long time ago. I did it for a while but it was too difficult after Joe came along."

"Your husband?" She shook her head.

"My son. He's 14." I was right about the yogurts.

"So, you living around here, or..?"

"Moseley."

"Cool." I nodded, I was calming down. "So, do you work in Town?"

"No, at St Mary's in Sutton. I'm a nurse."

"Right. I'll know who to come to next time I get a burn off one of those things," I said looking over my shoulder at the large rotisserie ovens. She laughed.

"I haven't worked in A and E for a long time, I'm in Oncology." I had no idea what that was.

"Cool. So do you still see anyone from school?"

"Not really. I see Becky Hadley sometimes. You?"

"Paul Lancaster and Rob Matthews sometimes. Actually quite a few people still go down The Brewers' on a Friday night; you'll have to pop down." And just like that I asked her out, sort of.

"Oh, I'd love to, but.... I'll have to see. My shifts are pretty erratic and there's Joe."

"Yeah, course." She'd hardly changed at all. She still looked amazing. I wished I wasn't wearing a white trilby hat. A call came from the kitchen.

"Martin." It was Carl.

"Just a second," I replied, "I'm with a customer." Happy with how confident I sounded I turned back to Rachel. "We

29

could make it another time then, if you want."

"Ok, we-".

Carl burst through the doors.

"No Martin, Dennis wants you upstairs now. He's put three calls out already, weren't you listening? There's a bloke from Head Office up there, they're waiting for you." I glanced at Rachel and she smiled back looking a little embarrassed. "Steven can you serve this young lady please," said Carl with the smirk of a slimeball. "They want you now Martin. There's been a Section 106."

Chapter Three

I was once told on a food hygiene course that you are more likely to contract food poisoning from dirty cutlery than you are from out-of-date or under-prepared food. Because of this I was always meticulous about cleanliness on the OC: utensils were washed three-times daily; ovens scrubbed nightly; and the entire floor space, including behind the fridges, was disinfected twice a week. On one food preparation exam at the Coventry Conference, I scored a class high of 96%, and I had mild flu that week. In my time as supervisor I'd only ever had a handful of complaints from customers, and none of them were ever up-held by management, so when the Council health inspectors said they were investigating a Section 106 against me I honestly couldn't believe it.

"You've got to understand, it's not against you Martin, it's against Thompson's," explained Ian Dent, from Head Office.

"And it's against this branch of Thompson's, my branch," fumed Dennis from behind his desk.

There were four certificates on the wall behind him. Three for Store Manager of the Year 1996, 1998, 2002 and one from Children in Need thanking our branch for donating £5,238.87 from last year's Staff Family Fun Day. Next to the filing cabinet was a list of emergency phone numbers and a solitary goldfish swam in an oval-shaped bowl. As I sat there I wondered if the fish had a name or just went by the initials

GF. On the shop floor Sting's Fields of Gold was being played on pan-pipes before the new company jingle sounded out across the aisles:

"Better choice, better value, better shop at Thompson's". It was a more up-market approach than the last one that had traded on the store's nickname in an all mates-together-type of way:

"Whatever you're after, you'll find it at Thomo's", like you were popping round for a barbeque or something. I should have been paying more attention but I'd tuned-out.

"She was taken to hospital on Friday night and diagnosed with salmonella on Saturday morning," Ian explained.

"The press'll have a fucking field day," moaned Dennis, "I've already had the local papers ringing up."

"How is she?" I asked.

"Bad," said Ian.

"Very, fucking bad," added Dennis. Something obviously told him he wasn't going to be named Store Manager of the Year 2005.

"She's in intensive care. They're doing tests but it doesn't look great at this stage."

"If she gets out of ICU it'll be a bloody miracle," Dennis added.

"What's her name?" I asked meekly.

"Elaine Baker. She's 72. If she was a bit younger it might be different," Ian continued. At least he seemed fairly calm.

"Why do they think she got it from here?" I asked. Had I honestly nearly killed someone?

"She bought a three-pack of chicken thighs on Thursday

afternoon. She had one for dinner and was on death's door the following morning. The health inspectors phoned us an hour ago."

"I can't believe it," I said, genuinely shocked.

"Salmonella," said Dennis, "This is bad. It sticks in people's minds. Look at Edwina Curry. This is bad for the whole company."

"Let's not get ahead of ourselves Dennis. We don't know anything yet." Ian had a cool head. He was Area Manager already and he was at least three years younger than me.

"That's right," I protested. "You know how clean my kitchens are, it might have come from the packing farm."

"They're checking there as well. But in the meantime we'll be suspending operations until the investigation is complete."

"We'll never keep this quiet; it'll be all over the news by tonight," Dennis blurted out.

"That's for our Comms Team to worry about. In the meantime I've called a staff meeting for this afternoon, where I'll be notifying everyone," Ian went on. "The Oven Counter staff will be moved to other departments for the time being."

"Ok." I said, feeling more at ease. So I'll go back onto the floor for a while, that's fair enough.

"Martin, Head Office aren't happy. Dennis is right, the press will be all over this and as a company we need to be seen to be taking a responsible approach." Ian was sounding less friendly.

"Ok."

"As Head of the Department, I'm afraid the buck stops with

you....?

"And you're suspended until further notice," Dennis butted in almost gleefully.

"Just until this all blows over," Ian added.

"You're suspending me?"

"With full-pay. But don't look at it as a suspension. I've been looking at your record, you've been with us a long time and we value that. Look at it as a chance to step-off the treadmill, recharge your batteries and hopefully this will all blow over."

"Not if she carks it," interjected Dennis, looking like he was willing it to happen.

"You've done this," I cried. "You've been waiting for a chance-"

Ian stepped in. "Let's not make this worse than it is."

"I've done this? You've poisoned an old woman."

"Dennis!" Ian barked. And the room fell silent for a few seconds.

"Martin, no one is out to get you. This isn't a witch-hunt."

"I'll appeal," I said, sounding pathetic.

"Then appeal, but the suspension remains in place."

"When does it start?"

"Effective...immediately," Dennis said like he'd been rehearsing it.

"So that's it, after 15 years, I get stabbed in the back?"

"Please Martin," Ian said. "Look at it from our point of view; this isn't just about you, this affects the whole Thompson's Family." No wonder he was Head Office, the corporate wanker.

And it was from that point that I stopped listening. That was supposed to be their thing at Thompson's; you weren't an employee, you were part of the family. Bullshit. Or if it was true then Dennis was the sadistic stepfather who chose his favourites and cast the rest aside. I felt like a renegade New York cop, hung out to dry by the bureaucrats at City Hall as I handed in my security card, white coat and trilby hat. I was given the statutory 20 minutes to gather my personal effects (my coat and bag from my locker) before I was shown to the door. As I left the office Ian told me how sorry he was and that I'd be notified as soon as there was any news. Dennis took a last swipe at shattering what was left of my dignity. "Maybe you're just not cut out for serving hot chickens," he mocked. But in a way it was the only sensible thing he had said all morning. I wasn't cut out for it, just like I wasn't cut out for law, or finance or marketing. As I stepped back out into the rain, I felt close to tears. I was 33 years old and no further along than when I was 13, but at least then I'd had hope for the future.

Chapter Four

After roaming the streets for the rest of the day it was nearly 4.30pm by the time I got home, changed and left again to meet Linda. It was dark and cold and I could hear a bombardment of late fireworks being set off by kids in the allotments.

"I hate this time of year," I mumbled as a blast of cold wind hit the back of my legs. "Dark when you get up, dark when you get in."

After years of cold mornings, waiting for trains in the rain, I'd had enough.

"This time I'm gonna do it," I said under my breath. "No more excuses." The idea came to me years ago while I was watching an Australia Special of Wish You Were Here. Judith Chalmers went to Sydney and the Great Barrier Reef, while some other bloke went to Western Australia. It was then that I saw Perth. Beautiful, perfect Perth. 38 degrees in the summer, 20 in the winter. Beaches, islands, everyone had a boat. I remember him saying that Perth was one of the most isolated cities in the world and after living all my life in the land-locked Midlands, where everyone was on top of each other, where one dreary town leads into the next, that was something that really stuck with me, the space, the isolation.

"Fuck England, fuck Thompson's, fuck the Council and fuck their fucking health inspectors. I'm doing it." I spat as I crossed into Garden Avenue and headed down along the

37

parked cars.

"This time I've gotta do it." God I hope I do.

I never really gave much thought to the mugging from day-to-day but as I approached the alleyway, the memory was strong enough to push everything else, Australia included, to the back of my mind. I was still 50 yards away when my left hand moved instinctively from the warm confines of my trouser pocket and up into my jacket. As I reached Sam Hedges' old house, I slid my middle finger through the metal ring on my keys like a knuckle-duster and clenched the long Yale key in my fist like a knife. Without even knowing it, as I approached the gully, my back and shoulders tensed and I felt my weight shift onto the balls of my feet. In another street a firework exploded and filled the air with sparks and sulphur and as I came within a car's length of the entrance I stepped out wide towards the road. A foot away and as my fingers gripped tightly around my keys, alarm bells sounded and adrenaline surged throughout my body. Fight or flight: get battered or leg it. All those years later and as I turned into the alleyway in Park View the hairs on the back of my neck still shot up instinctively. In my mind I saw his cut lip and blackened eye, the knife in his long fingers, the crazed desperation on his pale face, the stench of his breath as he leaned towards me screaming. But as ever, there was nothing. As my eyes adjusted to the low light I couldn't see a soul. It was always that way or if there was someone it was an elderly lady or a woman behind a buggy. No figure in black waiting against the railings, no calculated ambush. I stepped into the empty alleyway and as always my pace was brisk and my senses were alert until I reached the well-lit safety of Tudor Drive. Crossing between the parked cars my shoulders dropped and I slowed from my near-jog. I released my keys and as my hands slid back into my cosy trouser pockets I wondered if you could get Premiership football in Perth. I was really going this time.

I phoned Linda from the train to say I'd be able to make it a bit earlier but didn't explain why. She was pleased but her apparent surprise upset me a little. Did I really let her down that often? Linda, Craig and the kids were going to meet me at the cemetery but they would be leaving early to visit Nan. She asked me if I wanted to go too but I still couldn't face it, hospitals made me feel ill. The smell, the pity, the hushed whispers and solemn faces have a physical effect on me. They turn me weak, and angry, and upset. My Dad was only in hospital for six hours before he died, but it seemed like centuries. Everyone told me what a fighter he was, that he'd pull through, that the doctors were doing their best. Thinking about it, I couldn't believe how much could change in six hours.

"You haven't forgotten it have you? I rang you pacifically," Linda whined when I arrived at the cemetery. It always grated on me when she got words wrong; it made her sound stupid, which she wasn't. She'd become worse since being with Craig, the influence of his cadence coming through. I didn't say anything though, I'd learned from all the dead arms she'd given me in the past.

"I'm really sorry," I said. "I just completely forgot. I've had a right day." Between poisoning a pensioner and destroying 87

39

years of Thompson's retail I'd forgotten to phone Paul to borrow his strimmer.

"Can't you phone him now?" she asked.

"I tried on the way over, there's no answer. He might have gone to see the kids."

"Well what are we supposed to do?"

"I don't know, can't we just pull the weeds out?"

"I'm not getting all dirty, I'm going up the hospital in a bit."

"I'll do it then, you've done enough." In an hour they'd done bugger all.

"Oh, cheers Mart," chipped in Craig. He was the only other person who still called me Mart.

"Well you'd better not do half-a-job, I'm not having Mom-"

"I'll do it," I cut in. "I don't want her seeing it like this either." It looked like one of those sad graves that no-one cared about.

"Mooooooom. I've lost my hat," called one of the kids from behind a gravestone.

"Come here you two," Linda shouted back. "Put that down!" she barked, marching over to Michelle who was holding a watering can.

"Oh cheers Mart." Craig said, repeating himself.

"It's fine."

"Mart?" He said just as Linda walked out of earshot.

"Yeah?"

"You couldn't do us a bit of a borrow, could you?" He'd got that phrase off the telly. I think he thought people found it harder to say no to.

"No. Not again."

"It's just that I'm a bit short, you know, with Christmas coming up."

"You still owe me fifty quid from last time. What do you need it for?"

"There's a bit of a dead-cert that's come my way."

"A *bit* of a dead cert? It either is or it isn't. And what's that got to do with Christmas anyway?"

"If it comes in I'll be able to buy something nice for Linda and the kids. And pay you back, you know, with interest."

"How much?"

"Two-fifty"

"Two-fifty?" I can do you one fifty, but I need it back next week." I could be out of a job by then, I thought.

"Cheers Mart. I'll pop over tomorrow night, yeah?"

"Fine," I sighed, already regretting it.

"Bloody come here," Linda yelled. She'd found the missing hat but one of them had poured water over the other.

"Have you sorted things out for the anniversary wake?" she called back to me.

"Yeah. Work are doing the food, you and Dave just need to sort out some money for drinks. Do you know who's coming?"

"Most of Dad's lot, except Auntie Elsie, her feet are still playing up. Oh, and did I tell you Auntie Maggie phoned? Uncle Joe's back in rehab."

"Back on the booze?" I asked.

"Apparently. He sold the telly and disappeared for three days. He was found passed out in a car park; the police had to ring Maggie. He'd gone from pub to pub buying everybody drinks until they threw him out for kicking-off with someone. Anyway. We're off."

"Ok. Give my love to Nan."

"I will, I'll tell her you'll be in to see her this week?"

"Thanks."

"Come on you two. Cheryl, put her down."

"Cheers Mart. See you tomorrow, yeah?" Said Craig under his breath.

"Yeah ok."

"What are you two whispering about?" said Linda, looking suspicious.

"Nothing," I said. "Craig and I were just discussing your Christmas present."

"Ah. Come here you. You're dead romantic sometimes, you know that?" And she kissed him on the head. Forget Paris or candle-lit dinners, scrounging money off your suspended Brother-in-law to stick on a three-legged mule is true romance.

"See ya Mart. Come on you two," she called out into the darkness, "Or the ghost will get you."

"Don't tell 'em that," I told her. "You'll give 'em nightmares." Linda was in a playful mood now.

"Why Mart, scare you does it? She might get you. Everyone knows they never found the body." And she did a creepy Dracula laugh as she climbed into the car. I waved as they pulled away and watched the lights disappear behind the church before turning to the grave.

"Hello Dad. Long time, no see."

I spent over an hour at the graveside, feeling pretty ashamed of myself. Beside my Dad's was a beautifully kept plot with newly laid flowers and a little fence around the border. Most of them were like that, a neat and tidy place of remembrance where the memory of a loved-one lived on. My Dad's was a disgrace. The flowers were dead, and overgrown weeds spilled out towards the neighbouring grave. Looking at the filthy white marble headstone I noticed the numbers from the start of his date of birth were beginning to peel away. He'd been dead 20 years but it looked like he was already forgotten. The truth was, the anniversary would probably be the last time we made a fuss. Reaching into the long grass to pull out an empty crisp packet I felt guilty to have neglected his grave for so long, but then so had Dave and Linda. I finished cutting back the grass with Linda's garden sheers and set to work on the weeds. I hacked-away in silence. I'd been here when Mom or Linda had talked to the grave as if Dad would hear, but I couldn't bring myself to do it, I just didn't know what to say. If he'd been into football I'd have talked about the Villa or if he'd watched films, I'd have told him what I'd seen at the Showcase that week. But I didn't really think of him as a person anymore, just a cardboard cut-out of a Dad who popped-up in photos and the odd scattered memory. I hardly knew him, so I didn't really miss him. I felt guilty for thinking that as I dug away at the weeds while his body lay beneath me, but how was I supposed to miss someone I couldn't really remember? I stopped for a moment to blow warm breath into my freezing hands. God it was cold and I could barely see a thing under the distant streetlights. I had to work hard to loosen the undergrowth to wrestle the weeds out of the frozen soil, and after standing for an hour in the wet grass, my trainers and socks were soaked.

"Fuck," I said out loud watching my breath spill out into the bitter cold air. I carried on working. "Fucking suspended," I chuntered as I squatted down and tore a handful of grass out from beside the headstone.

"Did you hear that Dad? Suspended. Effective immediately. Is that how you thought your son'd turn out?"

I jabbed Linda's chrome-handled trowel into the ground. My wet feet were so cold my toes were numb.

"What'd you think Dad? Your son is such a fuck-up that some old lady could end up dying?" I dropped forwards onto my knees and stabbed the trowel into the earth again, hopelessness taking over.

"What am I gonna do?" I whimpered, plunging my left hand knuckle-deep into the mud and angrily tearing up a huge clump of grass.

"Fucking Dennis," I swore as I stabbed the trowel deeper into the ground, tears welling-up in my eyes.

"That fucking place," I said, striking the ground again.

"Fucking salmonella!" I cried. I leant forward to put my full weight behind the trowel but slipped on the wet grass and drove it into the back of my left hand.

"Fuuuuuuck," I screamed, and in a single motion stood up and threw the trowel full force into the distance. It hit something in the shadows.

"Damn it." I put my thumb in my mouth, it wasn't bleeding but it was already swollen and hurt to move.

44

"Fuck it. That's it," I shouted and picked up the shears and shovel to leave. My hand was throbbing. I walked over in the direction I'd chucked Linda's trowel but it was too dark to find it. Resigning myself to making an early start the next day I carried the rest of the tools over to the church where I stashed them out of sight behind a thick holly bush. I wanted to be at home watching a DVD. I wanted to eat a takeaway and drink a four-pack of beer. I wanted to fall asleep on the sofa and finally put an end to the day.

Chapter Five

Monday December 22nd 1975

It was just before Christmas and Dave and I were out playing. We were in the back garden wearing our coats and hats and it was nearly teatime. I only have the vaguest memories of that garden. Finding snails in the rockery, running through cobwebs that hung from the tree, losing footballs over the hedge and squashing ants by the back step. I was three at the time and if it hadn't been for what happened that day I wouldn't have remembered it at all. It would have existed, I would have got up, had breakfast, played all day, had dinner and a story before bed but I would have no recollection of it. As it is, it's probably my earliest memory, my youngest eventful day. Mom was in the kitchen washing up, occasionally looking up to see us play. Dave and I had three garden games for most of our early childhood; Cowboys, Army or Stuntmen, and as the eldest he always chose the game. We'd go out the back and he'd tell me what we were about to play and what my role would be (an Indian, a Corporal or a Stuntman's friend). As the years passed and the gap between us felt less significant I would argue that it was my turn to choose and if he let me I would always choose Army as it was the one game that meant we were both on the same side. We would always be Americans fighting an anonymous foe we called The Baddies. We had toy guns and talked in American accents like they did in films. I would usually die first, shot down as I naively tried to storm the enemy encampment in our Dad's shed. It was my lack of patience that was always my undoing. Dave played a waiting game, a considered assault on our intended target at the bottom of the garden. He liked the realism of creeping up on The Baddies, of planning an attack.

We didn't play Army that day, we played Stuntmen. It was my least favourite as it had less of a story than the other games. We didn't have characters we just practised stunts. Again we adopted American accents as we climbed onto the shed roof, or jumped off the pile of crazy-paving slabs in the corner. We'd also had a new climbing frame that summer and would incorporate it into our games as often as our imaginations would allow. I don't remember why I was on the climbing frame during that particular game. In the years that followed it would be a helicopter or the Millennium Falcon but that day I think it was just a climbing frame. Up the ladder and onto the monkey bars I scrambled and in a moment of brilliance I threw my legs up, passed them inside my arms, flipped 360 degrees and landed on the grass.

"Did you see that?" I asked Dave excitedly.

"What?"

"I did a flip."

"Do it again."

Proud and more than a little astonished by what I had done I scrambled back up the ladder, took position on the monkey bars and dangled my legs towards the ground.

"Are you watching?" I called out and without a moment's hesitation I repeated the stunt. Arms wide, legs up, but this time I slipped. My hand came away and I hit the grass three-feet below. I cried out and my Mom appeared in seconds and carried me into the house. I'd never known pain like it. The sharpness: the relentless stab of agony. I was placed on the sofa and covered in a blanket. Dave came in to make sure I was ok before going back outside to play. My foot hurt so badly but at the same time I felt stupid, a feeling I had probably not known before. My Dad got home from work and once they'd dropped Dave and Linda at my Nan's, my parents took me to hospital where I was x-rayed and was told I had a broken foot. Laying in the large hospital bed the pain eventually passed and I enjoyed having the sole attention of my Dad, as well as the smiling doctor and the nurse who set the plaster cast around my foot, ankle and up below my knee. She told me that I could get people to sign it but I didn't really know what she meant and didn't really like the idea of people writing on my leg. I was given the smallest pair of crutches they had in the hospital, but they were still too big for me.

"You need to be more careful, you can't keep jumping off things", my Dad frowned at me affectionately, patting my leg. The trouble was, jumping off things was one of the things I liked doing the most, and my Dad knew that. Unable to walk very far, trips to the shops or to my Nan's meant I had to go back in my pushchair and I was well aware I was too big for that. Dave said it was like I was a baby again and I remember an overwhelming feeling of frustration that the whole thing was partly his fault for not seeing the stunt the first time. I'd expected that Christmas to be full of adventures in the snow; Dad had promised to take us sledging and I was looking forward to snowball fights with Dave and Linda. Instead I had to stay indoors, sitting in the lounge, watching the others have fun through the window. At least my Dad sat with me when he was home, reading stories and playing games. I kept the cast for years after it was removed. The signatures, drawings and messages I eventually allowed faded and the side where it had been cut open began to turn to powder. I was probably 14 before I finally threw it away.

So it was an eventful day, one of excitement and agony, my earliest memory. I told the story of my broken foot (or leg as it was often exaggerated to) throughout my childhood. "Have you had any broken bones?" I'd ask other children on the playground or away during Cub camp. Like the numerous scars I collected from falling off my bike or out of trees, I liked the fact that I had evidence of my brushes with danger. It felt tough, purposeful; it said I was a 'man of resolve'. My first 13 years were full of action and adventure until the idea felt too much like hard work. As computer games and music filled the void left by scrabbling onto a garage roof or building a BMX ramp, my lust for excitement became something I used to have.

So in many ways my earliest memory was also my most significant. It was a time when the small back garden at number 23 Vicarage Road was a jungle to be explored or a new planet to be colonised. A time when my older brother and I were never closer and when help would come running out at a moment's notice, wearing Marigolds to carry me safely onto the settee.

Tuesday November 8ᵗʰ 2005

The joy of not getting up for work is soon dampened by the prospect of hours of daytime TV. Game shows, chat shows, cooking segments, gardening advice, makeovers for the home, makeovers for the wardrobe, phone-ins, quizzes too easy to get wrong, interviews with a model-come-actress-come-pop star that you fancy but she's 'here to play us out' so she won't be on until the end. It's enough to make pulling a sickie feel like work. By the end of This Morning it's lunchtime and the worst of the day is behind you and you probably should have gone in anyway. The dilemma comes later though. Do you go in the next day or take it off as well to validate today? At least that wasn't a problem I had because I wasn't off sick; I was suspended. I could walk around town without pretending I'd been to the chemist for some cough sweets. My love/hate relationship with days-off began at a young age. TV was different then but the result was the same. The Sullivan's, Country Practice, Take the High Road, Sons and Daughters and by 4 'o clock your mates would be playing but 'you can't go out if you've not been to school'.

I'd slept badly and woken up only mildly less angry than I'd gone to bed, my sore hand now complemented by a sore head. Laying on the sofa watching Trisha only made my mood worse. Where the hell did they find these people? 'My husband left me for my religion'. 'My husband left me for my neighbour'. 'My neighbour left me for my husband'. People so desperate for their 15 minutes that they didn't

51

mind what they said in front of who. At least they weren't as bad as the American ones though. I always thought there must be signs there outside the studios; 'No guns, knives or cameras and please leave your dignity at the front entrance for collection later'. White trash, red necks, hicks and hillbillies. People from trailer parks going on TV for the entertainment of people from trailer parks. But then who was I to criticise? It was 11 o'clock in the morning and I was dressed in socks, boxers and an old black t-shirt. Why was I so much better than some bloke on the telly? And I'd given some poor woman salmonella. As I pulled on my jeans I wondered how she was. Should I send flowers? What would I say? 'Get well soon and I'll fix you up with a month's free chicken wings.' I walked back into the lounge just as Janet from Bradford revealed her new makeover. She twirled in front of the camera to a ripple of applause. Maybe I'd judged too soon, I thought, she actually looked loads younger.

Outside it was one of those early winter mornings that are as nice as summer in their own way. The air was cold but the sun was bright and there was a crispness to the leaves underfoot. It is hard to stay miserable on mornings like this, I thought as I left my road and turned up towards Erdington High Street. I had to return some films to the video shop in 'the Village' (Cobra, Jackie Brown, Requiem for a Dream) before I got to the cemetery and I'd planned enough time for the obligatory chat with the bloke behind the counter. "I'm just dropping these back," I told him, placing the films on the counter.

"Cool," he said looking up from a sign he was busy illustrating. "What did you think of Requiem?"

He always did this if he wasn't busy, it was like a test.

"Um, amazing," I said. "Heart-breaking really. One of those films that leaves you wondering if there is any point in existence, you know?"

"Yeah. Have you seen Pi?" he asked.

"Yeah, it's excellent, that's why I wanted to see Requiem, I missed it at the pictures because I was on lates." I only called it Requiem because he did. He carried on shading-in his sign so I thought I'd better come up with something.

"Wasn't Arronofsky something to do with the new Batman film once?"

"Yeah, before they choose Nolan to direct it."

"Cool."

"Yeah, it would have been awesome."

"Definitely."

"It's like the Kevin Smith Superman script," he said again looking up from his sign. "Hardly anyone's ever seen it but there's supposed to be this line where Superman puts on glasses, turns to Lois and says 'I'm Clark Kent'."

"Brilliant," I replied. It really did sound great, a nice twist on the original classic.

"But it didn't work out and it ended up being a Bryan Singer film."

"Shame it never got made, it could have been excellent."

"Yeah," he said. "Just goes to show how differently things could have worked out."

53

By daylight the grave looked even worse. To my disappointment the hour I'd spent the night before had barely made a difference, but with a deep breath, I drew up a plan of attack.

"Right. Finish the weeds, rake off the grass and give the headstone a clean," I said. "You'll be good as new in no time," I added looking down towards my Dad. I retrieved the tools from their hiding place and went looking for the trowel to finish the weeding.

"Now, where is it?" I muttered looking in the general direction of where I'd thrown it. Staring back from the adjacent row was a grey-white angel standing above a two-foot high marble platform. She was surrounded by a four-foot ornamental wrought iron fence. Surveying the ground I couldn't see the trowel anywhere and after looking behind several headstones and peering into a thick rose bush three rows back from my Dad's, I was about to give up and buy Linda a new one.

"Where can it be?" I said out-loud and tried retracing my steps.

"Hit my hand, threw it, it hit something, probably that angel," I muttered walking up to the statue. I read the inscription aloud: "Mary Miller. Born 1848, died 1885." Not the best innings, I thought. Feeling a few drops of rain on my hand I looked up to the sky, but apart from a wisp of cloud it was a clear, blue day. Looking past the statue I expected to see a sprinkler in action, irrigating a memorial bush, but nothing. Standing there I felt more drops and noticed that the side of the statue nearest to me was wet with rain. A metre wide shower of rain fell - and it was falling sideways. I watched the droplets hit the angel's arm and back, run down its leg and drip onto the grass below just like it would do in a normal shower, except this rain appeared out of thin air. However much I'd wanted to, I'd never seen a UFO, never heard a ghost rearranging the furniture or witnessed anything vaguely X Files-ish, so this was pretty unnerving, even scary. I remember standing there for a full minute watching the rain fall horizontally. It acted like ordinary rain in every other sense, it just appeared from nowhere. Above it was a mild November morning; below it was an April shower. Looking back I can vaguely recall wanting to dismiss it and carry on with the weeding. I suppose the joy of hindsight is that it reveals a potentially life-changing moment every second, some quite inconspicuous, others, like sideways rain, impossible to ignore. With no gate to use, I stepped over the grey-coloured fence surrounding the angel, and it was with real hesitation that I reached out with my left hand to touch the source of the rain. As the first few drops touched my skin I felt shivers and my body tensed, sensing danger. As I stretched forward I felt a cold breeze hit my hand as if I'd put it out of a window on a stormy day. A few seconds later and the rain began to fall more heavily, and as I inched slowly forward the sleeve of my jacket felt wet. Leaning further it was like a downpour. Another inch and the tips of my fingers disappeared. I jumped back and stepped away another five feet, stumbling backwards over the fence. I looked at my hand but it was fine, it was all in one piece. I touched my fingers and they felt as normal as ever. Looking around I hoped to see someone else who might have witnessed what had just happened, but the cemetery was deserted.

"This is stupid," I told myself, feeling embarrassed. "Things don't just disappear, I must have been mistaken, everything's normal." Except for the sideways rain. "My fingers didn't just disappear." I was beginning to convince myself, but I could still see the rain falling from nowhere. A million thoughts raced for pole-position but as much as I wanted to leave, I didn't move. My mind swirled around in circles, seeming to get stuck and clogging up the mechanics, preventing me from thinking clearly.

"My fingers just disappeared," I thought once more. No they can't have done. I needed to try it again.

"But what if they disappear and don't come back," I heard myself say. "It was your imagination. Nothing happened." But I couldn't suppress the need to know. Stepping towards the statue I looked straight ahead, my gaze fixed on the rain. My left arm was extended and my fingers were tightly wrapped around a branch I'd pulled from a tree beside the church. Three feet away and the rain hit my shoes. Two feet away and I felt the cold air. A foot away and the tip of the branch disappeared. I held it in place for a second before moving forward. Another step and another six inches of the branch vanished. It was really happening; I walked on until the three foot branch was barely five inches long, only it still weighed the same. My hand was the next to go; it disappeared up to my wrist. It was gone but it felt just the same. I dropped the branch and moved my fingers, I could feel them responding just as they should. I reached in and I'd nearly lost my whole arm, but I was too curious to stop. I was being fuelled by nervous energy, I felt hyper-alert; all of my senses were at their most focused. My elbow, my bicep, and my shoulder vanished and, as if I was entering water, I held my breath before plunging my head through the invisible opening.

"Oh boy," I cried as I pulled my body back. What on earth was happening?

I used to be an adventurous kid; I would climb the highest tree or cycle the fastest on a BMX, but not anymore. As an adult I would never swim out of my depth or catch a train without a ticket. I'd never taken a risk in my adult life, so it still surprises me now to recall the moment I shook my head, took a deep breath, climbed up onto the angel's platform and jumped in.

Chapter Six

Friday November 8ᵗʰ 1985

I landed face-first on Linda's trowel.

"There it is," I said, rubbing my cheek, but where was I? I sat up, resting my hands beside the statue. It was properly raining now and as I got to my feet my jeans were soaked across the backs of my legs. I looked up at the grey clouds and thought about the clear blue sky I'd seen a moment ago. I glanced down at my injured hand and made a fist, it felt the same. I wiped the rain from my face and looked up at the angel as she peered solemnly out across the graveyard. Mary Miller. Born 1848, died 1885, the inscription still read. I picked up the trowel and bodged it towards 'the opening'. The tip disappeared and I stood with my arm extended. I looked around, the cemetery was deserted. I wondered if I'd fallen into a gap between days, a no-man's-land between yesterday and today. I wondered if I was the only person here, left behind while the rest of the world continued in the present. I pulled the trowel towards me and watched it reappear. I stood in silence, wondering if the laws of physics still existed here. I banged the trowel against the statue and it made a sharp metallic clang. I looked at the falling rain and wondered if gravity remained the same. I stood up on my tip-toes and then down onto my heels. Everything was normal. I weighed-up the trowel before throwing it into the distance, it travelled about 30 feet and landed in the wet grass. I stepped over the metal fence to retrieve it but as I looked around my sense of unease grew. It was hard to register at first, like my memory had betrayed me and it had always been like this. Where were the houses that backed on to St Johns Road? Where were the cars that had been parked up by the entrance as I came in? The contrasts were subtle, like a life-sized spot-the-difference and I was stood there trying to circle all the changes. Where had that shed come from? Where were the flats? Where was my Dad's grave? I stepped over to where it should be but the ground was grassed over, undisturbed. I jumped the fence, ran back to 'the opening' and forced my hand through, it disappeared. I pushed my face through and there was blue sky, dry grass and a headstone with my father's name on it. Back in the rain I looked down the hill towards the junior school. The third and fourth year blocks were gone, replaced by two mobile classrooms. I stepped away from the angel. I felt like I was spinning. I wanted to scream or cry or do something. I walked 20 paces before I stopped and threw-up. I coughed and caught my breath and looked down at the porridge I'd eaten while watching Tricia, it steamed in the rain. I bent forwards and dry-retched. The smell of sick made my stomach turn again and the acidic taste burnt my throat. I heard footsteps from behind the church and I shot around, the hairs on the back of my neck upright, my pupils dilated. An old lady appeared. My imagination ran into overdrive. This *was* the gap between times, the buffer between now and then, the void separating history and the present, a place where the last remnants of yesterday gradually disappear bit-by-bit. The old lady walked towards me. Then who was she?

60

Mother Nature? God? The physical manifestation of time itself?

"Are you alright bab?" she asked. She was in her early 60s and had a kind face. She was walking a toothless old dog that shared her umbrella.

"Err, yes. Err, no." I stumbled. "I feel sick".

"Do you need help?"

"Yes. I mean no. I mean, I think I'm alright. Where am I?"

"You're in the Cemetery," she replied.

"St John's Cemetery?"

"Yes dear."

"And. Are you Time?" I asked cautiously.

"The time? It's about one o'clock." I looked at my watch, she was right.

"No, that's not what I mean. I mean, is it today or yesterday?" She looked a bit nervous. "I know it was today but is it yesterday yet?"

She began to step away.

"Wait, just tell me where I am," I pleaded.

"You're in Birmingham bab," she said forcing a smile, her concern replaced with fear. "Anyway I'll just be-"

"And today? What day is today?"

"It's November the 8th," she said tugging at her dog lead in retreat.

"Tuesday November the 8th?"

"No, it's Friday." She turned to leave.

"Oh. I thought it was Tuesday." How is that possible, I pondered? "Are you saying it's Friday November the 8th 2005?"

61

"No love, it's still 1985."

I said nothing. She stopped and looked back.

"Are you from the hospital? Shall I…"

"How can it…" I trailed off too, my mouth dropping open.

"Which doctor are you under bab? Do you know his name? I can ring him for you when I get back, how does that sound?" She had slowed her voice, over-pronouncing every word.

"Please, this is serious. Are you saying it's 1985?"

"Yes dear," she sighed. "2005 is in the future."

"So this isn't a gap between times, a buffer between-"

"Do they know you're out?" she asked, her voice wavering.

"Who?"

"The doctors. They're probably looking for you."

"Looking for me? Nobody's looking for me. You think I'm crazy. Look at that rain, *that's* crazy. And the trowel…" I looked around. "It was here somewhere. It's Linda's, I threw it here last night…."

"Goodbye then dear."

"I haven't come from the hospital, I'm from… I work in the City, on the Chicken Counter. I'm not crazy, I'm from Erdington."

"Ok then Bab. I'd better get going then. Bye bye," she said as she turned and hurried away.

I watched her disappear from behind the church and breathed a sigh of relief. I was glad she was going, *she* was clearly insane. 1985? She scuttled further down the path, dragging her dog behind her, wearing the same beige C&A coat my Mom used to wear when I was at school. I took a second to try to slow my racing thoughts. I couldn't grasp what was real. I bit the nail on my right thumb.

Was I really here? Of course not. Then I finally figured it all out - I was dreaming. I'd had a lot going on with work and my Dad and the anniversary. It all made sense. It was a dream, just a very intense dream. The old lady was a cross between my Mom and my Nan, the dog a bit like the one my Grandad Richard had. The rain was my mood, the sickness the hangover after too much beer last night, the churchyard a strange mix of now and then, the date because I'd been thinking about the past. I started to calm down. My breathing slowed and the knots in my stomach unwound. I was at home, tucked up in bed waiting for the alarm to sound and drag me back to the present. But then why did everything around me feel so real? So familiar, like time had been rewound?

I looked at the cemetery, trying to make sense of what was happening. The newest looking grave stones were in a row behind me. I looked at the dates: 1925 – 1984; 1933 – 1984; 1954 – 1985; 1918 – 1985.

"No, it's still 1985," the old woman's words rang in my mind. I looked at the row to my left. There's got to be a more recent gravestone. There were people that had died in 1962, 1974, 1979, 1983, but no matter how long I searched there were no gravestones newer than 1985 and none with my Dad's name on them.

I walked towards the statue and was just about to go back home when I caught a glance of someone on the path leading up to the front door of the church. I ran around the

63

building and saw the back of a tall man approaching the door with a bag over his shoulder.

"Excuse me," I stammered.

He turned around to face me with a smile under a greying moustache.

"Yes?" He looked friendly. He was wearing a navy suit with a red trim and a matching hat. I glanced down at his bag and saw a pile of letters and parcels. Right, he was a postman, I could trust him to tell me the truth, I thought.

"Hi, yes, thanks. Erm…I was wondering if you knew the date please?"

"Yes, it's the 8th of November."

"Erm…sorry, yes, and the year?"

"It was 1985 last time I looked," he said, trying to make light of my strange enquiry.

"You're sure?"

"Yes," he frowned.

"Can you prove it?"

"What game are you playing son?" He suddenly looked less friendly. I started to back away.

"Sorry, that's fine," I said. "Just making sure you knew."

If reality is perception, I told myself, and our perceptions come from what we see, hear, taste, touch and feel then if something seems right then surely it must be - even if it's wrong. Of course I wasn't back in 1985 but everything, including the old lady and that postman, said I was. I stood beside the statue for what seemed like hours, but what was probably more like ten minutes. I don't know why I stayed. I don't know why I didn't just climb back through and carry on with my life. Looking back, part of me was too dazed to think straight, and another part of me was desperate to know what was going on. Of course it crossed my mind that 'the opening' might close, and I might get stuck in this strange reality, but something forced me to stay. I checked and rechecked that my world was still on the other side and made the decision not to go straight back. I wanted to know who was mad, them or me. As I left the cemetery the rain eased off and as I turned into Banks' Avenue, the sun began to inch through the grey clouds.

"I should have checked the weather," I thought absently as I walked along the empty streets. Nothing seemed right. I felt like Marshal Teller wandering through the streets of Eerie, Indiana. The houses all looked different but it took a while to put my finger on why. The gardens looked neater, the drive ways more uniform, net curtains in every window. The front doors seemed different too but it wasn't just the paint, it was the shape and style, all wood, no UPVC, and not a single double glazed window along the whole street. On the other side of the road I saw a woman walking behind a pram; one of the old style you imagine Mary Poppins pushing. Her hair was long and blond, and it caught the sun in a way that framed her face with a golden glow. A car drove by, radio blasting and window down. The big-haired driver was singing tunelessly about building a city on rock and roll. I found myself singing along, and noticed that the feeling of dread in my stomach was being replaced by a warm buzz of excitement. The car was a jet black Ford Escort XR3I. My Uncle Peter had one of those when I was growing up. A B-reg that he'd bought brand new. I'd never been in such a new car before and I remember how compact and sporty it looked, especially compared to my Dad's old Mazda, but as this drove by it looked big and boxy. The few other cars parked along the street looked the same. An Allegro, a Cortina, a Toyota Corolla Estate. Not a speck of metallic paint, no alloy wheels or Audi TT-inspired curves. I stopped at the corner of Castle Avenue and Exmouth Drive and said the words out loud: "This is 1985." But it failed to carry the impact you'd expect.

I used to stress-out a lot, too much really, at work and even when I was doing the things I loved. When you walk into the cinema the sign outside the theatre tells you what's showing. For a long time I couldn't relax before a film started. I'd go in, take a seat, listen to the Bee Gee's cover on the PA, do the movie quiz, unscramble the actor's name (Naff Bekcel = Ben Affleck), read the trivia and the whole time I'd question if I was in the right room.

"Of course I am, I read it when I came in," I'd tell myself. "But what if I'm not? Stuff it." I'd go outside and read the sign to check and it would always be right. So I'd go back in. Unscramble Donald Sutherland. Read about Ben Hur's 11 Oscars. Listen to Cher's Life after Love but in the background the doubts would emerge again.

"I definitely checked it right. But what if I didn't? What if Unbreakable was on next door and I read the wrong sign and I'm missing the start?" And this would go on until either the lights went down or I checked it again and possibly again. To this day I've never walked into the wrong cinema, but the unease remains. Yet there I was in the wrong decade and it was like I'd been time travelling my whole life. In fact, since leaving the cemetery, I could hardly keep the grin off my face. I felt slightly high, like the feeling after you'd been on a roller coaster, or stepped too close to a big drop. I felt different, different to how I'd felt for a long time. I was walking tall, striding confidently as I marched along the road, not really knowing or caring where I was headed.

My memories of the 80s, prior to around 1988 are at best fragmented. Going to school, playing football, making stuff off Blue Peter, watching Robin of Sherwood, going to the caravan, putting up posters from Look-In. There was music I wanted to like (The Smiths and The Jam) and music I liked (Culture Club and Dire Straits). These days the 80s are remembered for luminous socks and pink male dress shirts but in every photo of me prior to 1988 there's a lot of brown. My brown hair is side-parted and midway down my ears. I'm wearing brown jumpers, on top of cream coloured t-shirts with brown trim. But being back there I was surprised how much colour there actually was. I recalled a time of punks outside shopping centres, of smashed up red phone boxes and civil unrest reported on black and white tellies, but as the sun shone I considered that maybe it was my childhood that had been miserable and not the 1980s. "My God, I'm a kid here," I thought. I was 13. I'd been in the past for 40 minutes but hadn't considered for a second that I was in my past.

Apart from a few months back at my Mom's and the time at

Uni, I'd spent my entire adult life in Erdington. Like Salisbury has Stonehenge and Gateshead has the Angel of the North, Erdington is home to another national monument; the Gravelly Hill Interchange, aka Spaghetti Junction. As a feat of construction it is breathtaking - linking the M6, the A38 and the A5127 above two rivers, two railway lines and three branches of canal - but what it makes up for in civil engineering it more than loses in aesthetic appeal. It was supposed to put the area on the map, but even in Birmingham it's known by its pasta-inspired nickname. Everyday millions of motorists head towards Erdington from all over the country, before taking their exit and heading-off in another direction. My parents lived in neighbouring Sutton Coldfield, where I was now, two decades out-of-sync. Reaching the main road it seemed just as busy as the street I'd been on earlier that day, 20 years from now. Walking along I had no real idea where to go until I realised that without even thinking about it I was heading home. Fate was on my side and just as I looked up the 396 bus pulled into the bus stop ahead of me and I ran to make it just before the doors closed.

"How much to Park View?" I asked.

"14p," the driver told me.

I held out a 50 pence piece and on seeing his annoyed face, I pondered the fact that the five, ten and the fifty pence piece were all smaller reissues of the coins I'd known as a child.

"Funny money, eh?" the driver scoffed.

"Err, yeah. From France," was the best reply I could come up with.

"Can you change a pound?" I asked, reaching into my pocket and he sighed as he took the coin from me and counted out my 86p change. If he'd have looked closely he would have wondered why it said 2002 just underneath the Queen's chin but he didn't and chucked it in with the rest of the coins and pulled away.

Growing up in Sutton I was always aware what a different breed of people Suttonians are. Firstly, there's a lot of money in Sutton, a lot of big houses, private roads and BMWs. Secondly, although it's technically just another area of North Birmingham, some Sutton folk are very reluctant Brummies. The area was absorbed by the Second City in 1974 with the creation of the West Midlands county and the decision remained controversial 31, or 11 years, later. The boundary change saw Sutton lose its status as an independent borough of Warwickshire and become another suburb of Brum. Every so often the Sutton Coldfield Observer would report on calls for its independence but all the protesting in the world, it seemed, couldn't alter the past. Travelling through my old neighbourhood I recognised the changes. The chip shop I used to go to on the way to my Mom's was a carpet showroom and the place I got my hair cut last week sold car parts. Houses that I assumed had always been there had not yet been built, while others were marked by subtle differences like the lack of an extension, or only a single car on the drive way.

We lived in Mountfield Crescent until I was 14; I think Mom was just too sad there without Dad. I loved it there. I knew all the streets, the other kids, which neighbours liked you and

69

which ones would come out and tell you not to play near their house. I got off the bus by Mountfield News just as Mr Jackson came out with an advert for that day's Evening Mail. "Afternoon," he said.

"Afternoon," I said back, almost surprised he could see me. He was exactly like I remembered him, although I hadn't seen him since I used to go in and buy the Beano.

There was an old lady in the garden four doors down from our house. I recognised her immediately as Mrs Attlee; she was forever in her front garden. As I drew closer I remembered her nice face and the flowery patterned dresses she used to wear. She would always say 'hello dearie' to the kids that played by her house and as I passed I wondered if she'd say it to me, but instead of looking up and smiling like I should have, I couldn't lift my gaze off the ground. Seeing her standing there reminded me I was somewhere I didn't belong anymore, I was trespassing in my own street. I don't know how long I stood outside my house for, staring up at the bricks and paintwork, wide-eyed and hypnotized, but it was a long time. As I looked it came back slowly at first and then so quickly it almost knocked me off balance. It wasn't nostalgia though, I wasn't remembering the past, I was in it. Surrounded by everything I had known, and loved and eventually lost, a bombardment of memories, most I'd forgotten I ever knew, vied for centre-stage in my head. It was the smallest details that emerged at first. The grass seemed a little longer than I remember my Dad letting it get. The front door was green and used to stick sometimes when it rained. My room was on the left at the front of the house.

70

Dave's was on the right. I had a 96.4 FM BRMB sticker in the window that my Mom was forever telling me to take down.

My Dad was driving to Dudley on the day of the accident.

The boy next door was called Ben. He went to a different school. I heard he became a fireman. I once outlined a huge map of Britain on the driveway in coloured chalk and drew motorways and marked-off the places I'd been. We got snowed in one year and when it thawed the toilet pipe was cracked.

He collided with a lorry and had to be cut from his car.

My brother chipped his tooth when we had a water-fight on the front grass. We had a barbecue for my ninth birthday and I got loads of Action Force stuff. I got locked out after youth club once and Robert Ivy's Mom said I could go to their house for dinner.

He suffered head injuries, a broken pelvis, two broken legs, a ruptured spleen, a punctured intestine and a collapsed lung.

The man next door worked as a prison guard and had a punch bag in his garage. I used to climb out of my bedroom window sometimes and sit on the porch roof. We had a street party for Charles and Diana's wedding.

The lorry driver was admitted for shock.

Mark Haden's Dad built a BMX ramp in his garden but he only let fourth and fifth years use it.

The inquest was told his watch was damaged and stopped at the exact time of his death.

The ice cream van always stopped outside Joanne Cullen's house.

Even if he had lived, they said the brain damage he suffered would have been irreversible.

Gary Mason wrote 'Howard Jones, 85' on every lamppost in the road. I didn't play out for almost the whole holidays one Easter after Gary Stevens said he was going to batter me for cheeking his cousin.

My brother, sister and I went to live with my Nan for a month after the crash.

Standing in my street, in 1985, I had no idea how or why I had got there but if there was any clarity, it was in what I was going to do next. At 8.34am on Tuesday morning my Dad is going to be killed in a car crash and between now and then I'm going to stop it.

Chapter Seven

School kids were already at the bus stop by the time I got to Markham Road, they seemed so young and *Eighties*. They changed the uniform when I was in the fifth year to shirts and jumpers but in November 1985 it was still dresses for the girls and blazers for the boys. If it was 90 degrees in the shade and the concrete had begun to melt Mr Rawlins would sometimes relax the policy but otherwise they had to be worn at all times, including to and from school. If I'd have thought about it I'd have felt conspicuous, a 33-year-old bloke standing open-mouthed outside a secondary school with no justification for being there, but in the clamour of home time no one gave me a second glance. My mood had returned to an anxious uncertainty; I could feel my heart beating fast and hard against my chest. I wondered what would happen if I caught sight of my younger self, how it would affect me. Would it even be possible? What if it changed something in the tapestry of the Universe? What if time began to unravel? What if I created some sort of cosmic implosion? I was being over-dramatic, I told myself, I'd watched too many sci-fi movies; I needed to stop panicking. There was initially such an overload of faces that it was hard to train my attention on any one of them. Some were on bikes, one kid had a huge art folder, two fourth year kids kicked a football. I heard two girls talk about Mr Phelps, the Head of English, and another girl said she was getting the bus into Town, but for the most it was a din; an

indistinguishable blur of school bags and winter coats. I
focused my concentration, like trying to force a picture from
a magic eye puzzle, until eventually the images emerged.
Donna Taylor shuffled past wearing big glasses. I recognised
another girl in a blue scarf. Daz Watkins hurried by, brilliant
footballer, had trials for Blues. Stacey Taylor, whose brother
later went to prison. A stream of kids I didn't recognise then
Amy Walker, she was really nice. She works at the doctors'
surgery now on Oak Hill Road. Mark Walker, I think he
became a Maths teacher. Rob Booker, he runs the Park
Tavern. Mary Robbins, she was on the news a few years ago
when they were protesting against the Birmingham Northern
Relief Road. As I stood there, a crystal ball in hand,
remembering all these children's futures I was surprised at
how happy they looked. Most were laughing or chatting, glad
to be going home for the weekend. No money worries, child
care problems, mortgages or promotions to fret about. Just
making it home for tea and getting their homework done.
Michael Stokes nudged past me. He and I get drunk together
at Helen Baker's 18th birthday party in six years' time and I
puke on his shoe. Dean Farrell and Andy Regan crossed the
road in front of me. Dean Farrell will stick chewing gum in
my hair in assembly at some point. He might have already
done it. He works on Walsall market selling make-up now.
Chris Morrison was with Rob Morgan and Lee 'Banksy'
Banks. Morrison had hair like George Michael. I think he
does something in science now. Rob worked for his Dad
after sixth form. He'll be in the papers in ten years' time after
saving a boy from drowning in the sea.

I saw Claire Mansfield before I saw Rachel; the two of them were always together. Claire was wearing large hooped gold earrings that she must have put on in the toilets to walk home from school. Rachel was wearing make-up, her hair was loose and curly. She was so young. She could have been the daughter of the woman I served at work the day before. Rachel joined my junior school in third year primary. On her first day she had a massive scab on her face after she'd fallen off her brother's skateboard. Even then I liked that about her, that she went on skateboards. In class she had a pencil case from Orlando, Florida; but she hadn't been there, her aunt brought it back for her. In a way, she'd always been the one I've judged every girl by since, but before yesterday I'd hardly said a dozen words to her. Rachel and Claire were with Ben Woodgate and his mates, who were all fourth years. You could tell even then that Rachel could become an actress, not just because of her looks but she had a coolness and a confidence that made boys like me nervous at the thought of talking to her. They crossed over by the bus stop and Ben put his arm around her before they turned the corner and strolled out of view.

In the end, when it did happen, it was mundane and uneventful. There were no cosmic repercussions; no ripples in the fabric of reality. I was one of the last ones out that day. I came out by the sports hall on my own and crossed the car park near the main gates. I looked tiny, far too small for my rucksack. My shirt was untucked on one side and my hair fell forwards like I hadn't looked in a mirror all day. I couldn't believe how scrawny I was, how small and ill-

75

prepared for the big wide-world. Dwarfed by the buildings around me I past the science block and headed towards where I stood. If I'd begun my school reunion with some light-hearted voyeurism in mind, it ended the moment I arrived. I'd gone to school to eavesdrop on myself and my mates but standing there I was paralyzed with fear and disbelief. Instead of the warm sense of nostalgia I was expecting, being there felt unnatural and intrusive, like having an out of body experience and not liking the view. I saw myself as another person but with the harsh sense of criticism you can only apply to yourself. I was 13-years-old and small for my age. Shuffling along in my green Parka I looked like a sitting duck, easy prey for the Dean Farrells and later the Dennis Johnsons of this world. It was only a matter of time before I got chewing gum in my hair or was made the scapegoat for a woman's death. Looking at myself I saw exactly what that kid would become, a supervisor at an inner-city supermarket, and truthfully nothing had changed. I took a little more interest in my hair, if interest is what you call a grade four buzz cut every five weeks, but I still took the minimum interest in clothes and labels, investing my time and money on DVDs and computer upgrades instead. I might have had more girlfriends and the odd snog in a nightclub but nothing that kid would ever really aspire to. He looked down as he walked in front of me and I almost felt like apologising to him. If we could have talked, discussed our lives, I don't know who would have been more disappointed, him or me. I didn't know which one of us had the most to be ashamed of. I'd drifted along letting countless opportunities pass me by, but he set the whole fucking thing in motion. He becomes me, not the other way around. I used to blame a lot of it on my Dad and people let me, they still did 20 years later. People can't deal with death, they think it's the worst thing in the world so they submit to it and let you use it as justification for everything.

"Of course he failed his A-Levels, he lost his Dad."

"He's taking a break from university. You know, deep down I honestly think he's still grieving."

"He never got over his Dad. I don't think they do when they lose someone so young."

I'd heard it for years and willingly played along. Who could blame me? But there I was, four days before the crash looking at myself struggling to pull my hood up against the winter wind, and the die had already been cast. There's a picture at my Mom's house of me on a tractor on a farm, I think I was about eight. I looked so happy. I used to look at that picture and feel guilty because I had let that kid down, that I'd wasted all of his promise and ignored all of his ambition. But looking at that scruffy 13-year-old as he crossed the main road to join the group at the bus stop, I felt an enormous sense of relief. There was never any promise or ambition. It was as devoid in him as it was in me.

Chapter Eight

Tuesday November 8th 2005

It is said that if you look at anything for long enough patterns will emerge. That although the Universe is as infinitely small as it is infinitely large, if you study the chaos closely you'll identify order. In turn, if you learn how to read the order, from a mass of never ending possibilities comes a very limited number of outcomes and ultimately predictability. From research into the nature of sub-atomic particles at the end of a microscope, to the study of solar-systems light years away, what first appears to be random behaviour eventually reveals itself to be routine. Once the routine is established rules can be applied and from the rules scientists can formulate educated estimations on how things might turnout, usually based on the most complex theories and equations. Take the Australian soap opera Neighbours as a case in point. I hadn't followed it properly since the early '90s and because of work I could go months between each episode, but because I knew the formula due to years of dedicated research, I could pick-up the plot-line in a matter of minutes. Although the formula is an ever-evolving equation, the components remained the same. From the hum-drum of suburban Melbourne life (the chaos) emerges the routine. The constants (or characters) are varied but they are all central to a Neighbours episode or equation. The lead girl: cool, pretty, independent, assertive (typified by Charlene, Beth, Anne or Felicity). The lead man: cool, cute, troubled, sporty (think Scott, Brad, Dan or Billy). The father figure exists for the lead girl/boy to rebel against and/or confide in. First evident in Jim Robinson but consistent throughout the series' history. The constants go on. The wheeler-dealer to provide comic relief. The pretty/handsome temptation to test the lead girl/boy's relationship. The best friends, a just under par version of lead girl/boy. The sexy mechanic/gardener for the Mums. Then include situation; Ramsey Street, Erinsborough High, The Coffee Shop, and finally drama; teen pregnancy, family illness, cheating on the HSCs and it's a complete equation:

$N=D+SxC.$

The quality of an episode of Neighbours (n) equals the number of dramatic storylines (d) plus the number of situations (s) multiplied by the number of constants (c). The higher number of elements (drama, situations, popular characters), the higher the figure and the better the episode. Laying there on the sofa I smiled to myself for devising my first ever equation and concluded that even by taking maths into consideration, Neighbours wasn't as good as it used to be.

By the time I got home I caught the tail-end of kids' TV, said mentioned episode of Neighbours and was five minutes into a rerun of Friends when I started to fall asleep on the sofa. From school I'd caught the bus to the cemetery and after clamouring back through 'the opening', I re-entered the 21st Century. After checking four times that I could return I

walked down the alleyway, keys in hand, and stopped-off at
the cash-point before heading home, still feeling pretty low. I
would never have guessed that time-travel could be so
depressing. I fell asleep just as Chandler was trying to talk his
way out of a misunderstanding with his boss.
"Fucking Dennis," I thought as I folded the cushion in two
and shoved it under my head.

Friday May 16th 1980

My Grandad Richard, my dad's dad, died when I was seven.
He was a tall, well-built man with a barrel chest and a full
head of grey hair. He was 64 when he was taken into hospital
with chest pains and never came home. We visited him twice
in the days before his death and I remember asking him if
he'd be able to come to my school nativity play and he said
he'd try. Before the heart attack he was fit and active and
played golf with his old work colleagues from the garden
centre. He was 24 when the war broke-out and worked as a
motorcycle mechanic at Birmingham Small Arms in
Sparkbrook. He and my Nan, Jessica, lived in nearby Balsall
Heath and according to him, he signed-up for the Army on
his way home from work and told her about it over dinner.
"That's just how it was in those days," he told me, half
proud, half embarrassed.
He joined the Royal Signals as a motorbike dispatch rider
and was sent away the following week, leaving my Nan at
home with three children, including my two-year-old Dad.

He had all sorts of scrapes with death during his six years at war, and as children Dave, Linda and I would love sitting on his lap to hear all about them. My favourite was when his patrol was stranded in the Egyptian desert and they had to eat beetles and drink the water from the engine radiator until they were rescued six-days later.

After the war he remained in touch with his army pals and they would meet up a few times a year to go hiking in the Welsh hills, eager to put their fitness and navigation skills to the test. It was on one of his many trips to Snowdonia that he had his photograph taken on top of The Cantilever Stone, a strange, natural rock formation on the mountain Glyder Fach. It's a wonderful photo. My Grandad and two of his mates standing on the horizontal slab of grey rock that juts-out on the mountain's top. He's on the left of the other two and wearing an old army backpack, a black coat, red scarf and a blue and white hat, knitted for him by my Auntie. The sun is bright but low in the sky and the jagged rocks cast long shadows across the black and white landscape. On the back he had written *Tryfan '54* but there was no mention of the other men's names. Tryfan was his favourite of 'the hills'. He even met Sir John Hunt, the leader of the British Everest Team, up there one year. Hunt and three others were testing their equipment and my Grandad met them while he was on his way down and warned them about bad weather at the top. The photo was in a frame in my Grandad's workshop and it was always the one I liked looking at the most. When he died the photo went to my Auntie Emily and I never saw it again. My Dad also loved that photo, and it was clearly on his mind that day as we drove through North Wales to stay in a caravan in Caernarfon.

"Can you see? Up there. That's where your Grandad used to climb", he pointed out to me as we drove past the black, jagged outline of Tryfan in our car on the A5. It was a monster, a harsh, cruel looking mountain with bristles and edges jutting out at all angles. It looked like it had fallen from space, a black asteroid that had landed in the green, grassy hills. I couldn't imagine my Grandad clinging to the side of it, scaling its stony spikes until he reached the top.

The caravan belonged to a work colleague of my Dad's and was just outside of the main town, near to the beach. Linda and Dave had stayed at home. I heard Linda on the phone to Abi planning a party before we left but I didn't say anything, I just hoped they didn't go into my room. The site was peaceful and relaxing and while my mom sat on a deckchair in the sunshine, I explored the nearby woods with my Dad, or walked down to the chip shop to play the arcade machines. I would win sometimes, but I always knew he could've beaten me.

In the pub on our second evening I was just tucking into my Scampi and Chips when my Mom and Dad struck-up a conversation with the couple at the table next to us. He asked my Dad if we were having a nice time and the lady said how good and quiet I was, which made my Mom smile and my Dad wink at me. They were from Worcester and were younger than my parents. She had blonde curly hair and a floral dress and he had a crew cut and a square jaw, like an

Action Man figure. They were both teachers. Her name was Trish and she taught English, he was called Alan and he taught Science. It was when my Mom asked what their plans were for the week that Alan said he was going hiking in Snowdonia and planned to climb Tryfan. He had done a lot of climbing in the Peak District while he was at University in Sheffield, but had not been for a while because of work.

"Tryfan?" my Dad replied excitedly. "My dad used to climb that. I always wanted to go but he would never let us."

"Well come along," Alan offered. "Always glad of the company".

My Mom shot my Dad an icy stare.

"Really? You think I'd make it?"

As the evening went on and he sunk a few more pints of ale, my Dad became more and more excited at the prospect of following in his dad's footsteps and by the end of the night he and Alan had arranged to meet the day-after-next to climb Tryfan. We said goodnight to the others and drove home in silence, my Dad probably working out what kit to take, my Mom working out what she was going to say to stop him.

"You're not really going up that mountain are you?" she asked eventually once we were back and I was sitting in front of the telly.

"Is that why you're in a mood? Why not?"

"It might be dangerous."

As she turned to put the kettle on, he rolled his eyes at me in a conspiratorial fashion.

"Nonsense. My Dad went up there loads of times. You remember that old picture? He was about my age."

"I know, but he was a lot fitter love, you know, with the Army and all that."

It didn't quite escalate into a row but it came close. In the end my Mom must have realised that every attempt to talk my Dad round only cemented his resolve.

The next day we went to the beach and had a brilliant time. The sun shone and I built a huge fortress out of sand for my Star Wars figures. My Dad helped me with the finishing touches before he took control of Obi-Wan Kenobi and I controlled Luke. The mission was to rescue Chewie from evil droids and incorporated all of the ten figures I was allowed to bring with me in my old pump bag. As we battled the Empire my Mom read her novel, trying to blank out our cries and laser blasts. When it got to half three my Dad said he was going for a walk to build up some energy for the next day's hike and would bring back some shopping for tea. I wanted to go with him but Mom said I'd been in the sun for too long and that I needed to sit with her in the shade. When he was still not back at five thirty my Mom began to get worried, and by six 'o clock most of the families had packed up and headed home for the evening. I sat watching out for his return, not able to concentrate on anything else. He finally arrived at six twenty, a hobbling figure moving slowly across the sand. I spotted him first and ran over to see what was wrong. As I got closer, I could see an anguished look on his face.

"You ok?" I asked. "Mom said you've been ages."

85

"It's alright son, I've just done me back in," he replied through gritted teeth, shuffling along with a Buy-Co carrier in each hand. He looked older than I'd ever seen him, frail, like a gust of wind might blow him over.

"What happened?"

"Oh nothing, I'll be fine. Here, build up your muscles and grab one of these," he said, passing me a bag of shopping. We got back to my Mom and she helped my Dad into his chair.

"It's no good, it's gone," he said to her quietly. "Like when I was moving your Dad's fridge."

We packed up and Mom and I carried the shopping and the beach things back to the car, while my Dad hobbled along behind. He lowered himself into the driver's seat and managed to get us back to the caravan, where he headed-off to bed. I made some toast and watched telly and hoped he was going to be alright. My Mom went to the pay phone on the main road and left a message for Alan at the clubhouse of his caravan park to say my Dad wouldn't be able to make it. The next day, with the use of a walking stick, my Mom found in the wardrobe, he made it to the deckchair outside where we brought him tea and cakes and we spent hours playing battleships on the small camping table. By the following day he said it was easing up and by our last day he was back to normal. He said he would write to Alan to arrange things for next summer, I don't know if he ever did. I remember wondering years later if Alan and Trish ever found out about the accident.

When we arrived home Linda's party had resulted in a crack in one of the bathroom tiles and a brown stain on the living room wall. She was grounded for a week. Nobody mentioned my Dad's back so neither did I. That night when I closed my eyes I remembered looking up at Tryfan as we drove back, its black peak reaching up into the sky and thought how lucky it was that my Dad had hurt his back.

Tuesday November 8th 2005

I awoke to the sound of the doorbell. Friends had been replaced by the Channel Four News and I was freezing.
"Alright Mart?" Craig asked.
"Yeah, come in."
"Can't be long Linda's expecting me back for tea."
"Yeah, fine." I walked over to the coffee table and handed him the money.
"Aw, cheers."
"Remember it's a loan."
"Yeah, course. Don't worry it's a dead cert. They're paying 18 to one at the moment," he boasted.
"Doesn't that mean it'll never happen? That the odds are 18 to one *against* it happening?"
"Naw. You're a bloody glass-half-empty-type you are Mart. It means it's 18 to one in favour of it coming-off."
"But the long shots don't come off. That's the point," I protested.
"They do."
"When? Name one."

"Err." He looked around the room. "Err, the football…
Greece winning the 2004 Euros last year. Rank outsiders at
the start of the tournament, they beat Portugal one-nil in the
final."

"And did you bet on them?"

"Naw, I always bet on England. You know, to make the
victories sweeter."

"England never win anything. *They* were supposed to be a
dead-cert and they were shit, like always".

"Yeah, they should have won it though. Eriksson bottled it
and tried to defend a one goal lead, that's all."

I walked into the kitchen and switched the kettle on.

"Ok," I continued. "Name one rank outsider that you've
ever bet on and won."

"Er." He looked around again. "Wimbledon," he said with a
sense of achievement.

"What do you know about tennis?" I scoffed.

"Not the tennis, the football. I bet on Wimbledon to beat
Liverpool in the FA Cup."

"That was 1988. You weren't old enough to go into betting
shops."

"It was '87 and my Dad used to do a little bet for us. I put
my money on Wimbledon when Liverpool were the best
team in Europe."

"Why?"

"I hated Liverpool, they were like Chelsea or Man United are
today, everyone wanted to see them lose."

"And how much did you win?" I was actually starting to be
interested by this conversation.

"12 pounds."

"12 pounds?"

"It was a lot of money then," he stated. And he was right it was. Talking to Craig confirmed what an absolute idiot I was. Why hadn't I thought of this sooner? You hear the expression 'the penny dropped' but in my case it was 1,200 pennies.

"And what were the odds like?"

"Dunno, I was a kid. Good though."

"And what would they have been like at the start of the season?"

"Really good, Wimbledon had never made it to an FA Cup Final before, let alone won it."

"And what if you bet on them two years earlier?"

"Err…" He looked a little confused. "Well the earlier you bet, the better the odds. You get blokes betting their newborn son's gonna play for England in 18 years' time. They get really long odds, a hundred to one and stuff."

Now I was listening. Although I'd always gone to the football I'd never really gambled.

"Ok, let's say I wanted to bet, how could I get odds of a hundred to one?"

"Erm. Bet early and pacifically I suppose." I blanched.

"What? Not just the score?"

"Naw, you want the scorer, the times, the half time score, the first goal."

"I'd get a hundred to one on all that?"

"You'd probably get a thousand to one. But you'd never win, how could you guess all that?"

"But say you had a crystal ball and you knew the results, what would you do? How would you really make money?" He smiled, too excited by the prospect to wonder why I was asking.

"You'd keep it small, I suppose. Spread it around. Different races, different bookies, so you didn't raise too much interest." He saw my confusion. "They look out for the big wins to pass information to the police for match fixing and that sort of thing."

"Yeah?"

"Yeah. Well I'd build up a little nest egg for the Big One." He had the frenzied look of a seasoned gambler.

"Like what?"

"An accumulator over a year or two." He was almost salivating.

"That's a long time."

"Yeah but if you could get the winner of the National, the Derby, the FA Cup, the Champions League. The everyday, run-of-the-mill, BBC Sports stuff, then no one could accuse you of fixing. You know about Phil Frasier's uncle? He went down for-"

"And what'd happen if it all came in?" I cut him short. "The BBC stuff?"

"If you got all that? Dunno. If you stuck a thousand quid down you'd probably bankrupt the bookies." My jaw fell open at the thought of it.

"And Mart," he added. "You'd never have to roast another chicken in your life mate."

Chapter Nine

Wednesday November 9th 2005

I barely slept at all that night. I was online until late looking up tomorrow's racing results, circa 1985. I then made a list of 'the BBC stuff', and as well as the football and horse racing I put together the results of The Boat Race, the boxing, the Grand Prix, The Ashes and The Marathon. I even thought about having a flutter on Charles and Diana ending up in the divorce courts but given that they'd only been married three years, it seemed like I'd have a long time to wait. The rest of the night was spent formulating a plan to have enough 1985 currency to bet with. I initially considered going back and buying antiques to sell in 2005, but an extra couple of decades on a 250 year old dressing table didn't seem like such a big deal. Anyway, I knew nothing about antiques and might look suspicious lugging a chest of drawers around a cemetery. Thinking back to that day on the beach with my Dad, I eventually found inspiration from Obi-Wan Kenobi, and dug-out my old VHS videos from under the bed. Despite having bought them all again on DVD, I'd kept my copies of Star Wars, Alien, Blade Runner and other Sci-Fi classics that would take years to come on the telly in 1985. I took the cassettes out of their boxes and removed any stickers that might give away their origin. I thought about taking back my copy of Aliens to sell as well but I remembered hearing this thing about the space/time continuum and decided against it.

Saturday November 9th 1985

There was a group of girls outside of Our Price. They were gently swaying to Marillion's Lavender, whilst trying to look nonchalant. In the window hung a massive poster of Morten Harket and a steady stream of customers headed out holding LP-shaped carrier bags. Our Price went to show how nothing lasts forever. Rome fell, Russia revolted, Britannia was left exhausted after two world wars and at some point in the 1990s, the chain lost its monopoly on the music-buying British public. In ten short years the popularity of the once dominant Our Price record token would sink faster than a depression-era dollar and would be worthless next to the emerging Virgin Voucher and MVC Discount Card. Further along the High Street, Tandy - the electrical store that specialized in all things Tandy - was already showing signs of decline. And from the window of the Midland Bank a friendly looking griffin smiled naively at passers-by, unaware that he'd be made extinct one day by the banking corporations of Hong Kong and Shanghai.

One establishment around in both time zones was The Trading Post, a grubby second-hand shop just off Birmingham Road. It had a dirty orange sign with faded black lettering that had not changed in twenty years. A metal grid was riveted to the wall and stretched the length of the front window and a sign on the front door read: 'goods bought and sold for cash'.

I approached the counter and coughed loudly to catch the attention of the owner. Midge Ure's If I Was crackled out of a Sony tape player. On the counter stood two black and white televisions and a Goblin Radio Clock Teasmade. A note next to the till said cheques were payable to The Trading Post c/o Derek Evans. Derek appeared dressed in a tracksuit, smoking a roll-up. I explained that I had some videos he might be interested in, films straight from the cinema. He was clearly suspicious at first, but after playing the first five minutes and fast-forwarding through to the end he was satisfied my consignment was legit.

"This is illegal you know," he said, talking in a hushed tone, even though there was only one other person in the shop and he was at the back looking at old fashioned radios.

"Ah, no," I protested. "They're not pirated; my mate gets them over from America. Look at the quality."

"They are good. I had a load of Kramer Vs Kramer in here last month and you could hardly see a thing. How much?"

"Two pounds."

"Two pounds *each*? I can't do that."

"You can sell 'em for at least three, The Terminator's only just been released.

"I'll give you one fifty. That's the best I can do."

"Ok," I sighed. I was sad to see my old videos go but it would at least give me the cash to get started. He piled up the cassettes and placed them out the back before counting out £21 and handing it to me.

"Can you get anymore?" he asked.

"Maybe. I'll pop back if I can."

"Can you get any on Betamax?"

"Err. Not sure."

He drove a hard bargain but seemed like an alright bloke so I thought I'd better warn him.

"Derek, is it?"

"Yep."

"Derek. If you've got a second, I've got a theory on Betamax videos."

I remember seeing this program about how they've done a lot to clean up bookies in the last few years, well in 1985, I realised why. Pre-satellite and long before The Racing Channel, results came in over the radio and were put on a scoreboard above the counter. With only 21 quid in 'old money' I made sure I bet small at first to test the system, but after Mile Oak romped home in the 11.45 at Chepstow, the gloves came off and the wallet came out. At £800 I thought I'd better start backing the odd looser to avoid raising suspicion. Just as Craig advised, I spread it about. £4.50 on Royal Blue, £2.30 on Caledonian Clover. I never thought my brother-in-law would prove so useful. After every third race I'd head to the toilet to check my print-out, rip up the last three results and send them packing with a grateful flush. I made over £5,000 that first day travelling between 14 different bookmakers. It was incredible; the fact that I knew the race results did nothing to taint the victory. By 3.30pm I was sat in The Cup celebrating with a pint and a packet of cheese and onion crisps. On my first morning I'd made more than enough to bet big on a five-leg accumulator and be set up for life. Everything was going to plan except there was still a bit of a question-mark looming over the whole scam.

94

Making the money was easy, but how did I collect it? I looked at my 'BBC list'. My last result was Liverpool beating Everton in the FA Cup in May, assuming 'the opening' stayed open that long. The problem was, when I raked in fifty million quid, how was I going to access it? Presumably the bookies would write me a cheque for my winnings but the only bank account I had access to in 1987 was the Nat West Junior Savers account I opened to pay my birthday money into. The only reason I knew it still existed was because it was included on the quarterly statements they still sent out for my current account. I tried to think it through. Even if I could get the money paid into the long-forgotten account, with three bets at different bookies the winnings would be huge and would earn enormous interest over the next two decades. It was unlikely I'd overlook the fact that I was actually a multi-millionaire. I finished my pint, ordered another and gave it some more thought.

"Right, I could write to the bank and request that they don't send statements," I told myself. "So I'll never know that the money's there. Excellent. But hang on. If I do that, then how do I know now that the account still exists? But maybe I know it exists now because I haven't changed history yet, so when I send the letter, it will change the past so that I wouldn't have had the letters, and I would lose the memory of the account. So maybe I need to find a way to remind myself about the account later. But then if I did manage to change the past, wouldn't my past be different now?" My head hurt. I looked up as some of the afternoon regulars began to arrive. A bloke stood at the juke box and a moment later 10cc's Dreadlock Holiday sounded out across the bar. "Yes. Ok." I had it. It would be difficult but doable. I ask the bank not to send out any statements until early November 2005, reminding myself that the account is still there. Excellent. I sat back and took another sip of my pint.

"But if I don't know the account exists before then why do I remember getting regular statements now?" Even if I tried to do it, it obviously didn't work. I knew there must be a way and my mind mulled over the possibility of setting up trust funds and off-shore holding. But in 1985 I was 13 and I was pretty certain they wouldn't let me open a Swiss bank account; I couldn't even save up enough money to get all the collectable piggy banks. I just couldn't work it out. Winning the money was no problem, the thousands of pounds in my backpack was proof of that, but how could I get my hands on it 20 years later? Even if I physically take it back with me it'd be worthless because the notes are no longer in circulation.

"That's probably why the Bank of England changes the money so often, to stop time travellers fucking with things," I swore under my breath.

I looked up at the blokes at the bar, chatting and enjoying a laugh. I thought back to last week when life seemed more straight forward, no suspension and no time-travel complexities to figure out. I finished the last of my pork scratchings, downed my pint and headed for the door.

Wednesday November 9th 2005

I caught the bus back to Erdington and was looking forward to getting home. I was starving hungry and hoped the chip shop would still be open. I also wondered if my plan, which was becoming increasingly elaborate, would ever work. I said cheers to the bus driver as I stepped down onto the curb. It was a warm afternoon for November and I felt calmer and more relaxed than I had done in days.

"Time is on my side," I told myself. I knew how it would all pan out and it was just a case of making a few minor adjustments to put everything right. My new optimism bought a fresh bout of clarity to my thinking and I was reminded of my last Thompson's Away-Days, the twice-yearly team-building conferences we were duty-bound to attend. We would devote hours to problem solving and task management exercises, and if nothing else, it was a few days off work and a night in a mid-range hotel. The first day was always an orchestrated meet-and-greet and we would all make small-talk over fizzy orange juice, wearing name badges to aid the introductions. I would often take a backseat during the initial proceedings, not because I didn't like Away-Days, but because I liked to suss out who was who. The junior management get-togethers every April were the best; 120 department supervisors from across the country gathered in Swindon for two days of blue-sky thinking and envelope pushing. Afternoons were always about team-building and would involve a practical challenge or some kind of a problem that had to be solved in small groups. A task that arose twice, albeit four years apart, was to build a device that could prevent an egg from breaking when dropped by a man standing on a chair. Each group was sent to a space in the room and handed a bin liner full of bottles, tins, Clingfilm, egg boxes (a major red herring), newspaper and cereal boxes. Twenty-five minutes later the groups stood proudly around an array of tubes, towers and tunnels carefully engineered with precision and sticky tape to catch and cradle the falling egg. My first group's attempt was a disaster, hijacked by a bloke called Tim from the Salford payroll team. With all our performances being reviewed he was playing like he had something to prove and right from the start he was obsessed with the idea of building a newspaper hammock. He was completely unwilling to consider any other method and we followed his plan only to see our egg splatter across the floor. We even lost points for our lack of group cooperation. As it was, all six eggs defied our inventions that day but after five pints in the bar that evening, Rob, our Away-Days trainer, let slip to a select few the secret of how to rescue Humpty from his 8ft descent.

Cut to April 2005 and seven minutes before the whistle was due to sound I acted like I'd hit on a brilliant idea. Marco, the newly appointed Durham branch fish counter manager, was unsure my plan would work and of the eight of us he had the backing of at least three others. Officially, we were not supposed to acknowledge the invigilator as she made her stealthy rounds but just as she appeared within ear-shot, clip-board in hand, I made my move.

"Look I hear what you're saying," I told Marco. "But I think it's important we reach a decision as a team." From the corner of my eye I saw her pause and make a brief note. "But I can't see how it's gonna work mate," he replied and a few others nodded in agreement.

"It'll work, just like it does in cars, but I think we should settle on a course of action and stand by it as a group." Again people nodded.

"Let's vote on it," I said confidently.

The invigilator scribbled a few more lines before moving on to the next team. My plan won 5-3 and with a minute to go I moved aside our nearly completed plastic bottle chimney contraption and replaced it with an airbag-inspired catching cushion made from the bin liner everyone had been given at the start and over-looked. Needless to say, the egg landed safely in the centre of the bin bag and as the air escaped from the loosely wound opening it was gently lowered to the ground. Some people even clapped and I pretended I'd seen a documentary on crash-test-dummies a few weeks earlier. At the Away-Days Awards I was named 'Most Innovative Leader', received a £100 Thompson's voucher and even got a mention in the next monthly newsletter.

With the ice-breakers out of the way, the second part of any Away-Day was less fun and more formal as we sat through seminars on improving life within the Thompson's family. Raising staff morale, dealing with awkward customers, disciplining members of staff, handling complaints, increasing sales, reducing theft, organising holiday rotas, training, promotions, inductions, appraisals, dismissals.

Every aspect of junior management was summarised, simplified and beamed across the room on an overhead projector. More recent seminars came via a power-point presentation, which were always curiously prefaced by the phrase: "You'll have to bear with me, I've never used one of these before". Whatever the topic though the key word for the second day was acronyms, and weak ones at that. Favourite among Away-Days trainers were TEWCs - Training Exercises without Customers. Fictional scenarios were given to us and we would collectively outline the best ways to deal with the situation. Like the egg game, the end result was secondary to how we reached it as long as we adhered to Thompson's GOLDEN rules - Good Objectives Legitimise Decisions, Even Negative ones. Or GOLDENO if you like. It didn't quite work but I understood what it meant and as I hurried home I pictured my predicaments on a flip-chart and imagined I was addressing a junior management seminar as Sonya, the trainer, looked on.

"Problem," I said. "I need to improve family morale by rescheduling past events." Sonya smiled at my use of boardroom parlance.

"Objectives," I continued. "To rectify issues leading to my father's earthly dismissal and increase personal profits through the use of sensitive market information."

"Excellent," said Sonya from behind her big specs. A hand shot up. It was Marco.

"So you wanna save your Dad and bring loads of money from the past back to the present. I see what you're getting at but I don't think it's gonna work mate."

My daydream paused briefly as I reached the pedestrian crossing on Station Road. Sonya was the first to resume. "Now come on," she said. "That's not the attitude." I past the Chester Arms and three drunken women fell through the front door laughing. I walked on, head down and transported myself back to the seminar.

"Thanks," I said acknowledging Sonya's encouragement and she smiled back. She wasn't even a genuine trainer, just an amalgamation of the many I've seen over the years. She was noticeably more attractive than the real trainers.

"Now priority one, my old man." I stepped into the road to avoid some scaffolding and imagined myself turning the flip chart to reveal a picture of my Dad.

"Now, can anyone think of a way Martin can achieve his objective?" Sonya asked the group.

"Nick his Dad's car," someone called out and a ripple of laughter spread across the room.

"Very funny but can anyone think of any legal suggestions?" Sonya was looking a bit cross.

"He could warn him," suggested a girl on the front row.

"Go on."

"Well, I don't know. Tell him about the crash, so it doesn't happen."

"And how, realistically could Martin do that?"

"He'd look mental," called out the funnyman from earlier and again people laughed.

"Well yes probably," Sonya agreed. "So how could he avoid that?"

"Write him a note," someone called out but Sonya shook her

head.

"And how seriously do you think he would take that? What would you do if you received an anonymous letter telling you that you were going to die in three days? No, try again. And this time try thinking outside of the box."

I gathered Sonya already had the answer; it was just a case of coaxing it out of us.

"See if this helps," she said glancing back to me. "Martin would you please?"

Taking her cue I turned the next page of the flip chart. The group gasped and the girl on the front row turned away as the image came into view, a police accident investigation photo of the crash. It was barely recognisable as being my Dad's car, more a devastated wreck of glass and metal. The group fell silent for a second.

"Oh damn it," I said breaking back to reality, the chip shop wasn't open yet. As I turned towards the crossing, I let Sonya continue.

"Now where does Martin's Dad not want to be on Tuesday morning?" she asked us.

"There," said the front row girl, pointing at the picture.

"Exactly. And how do we stop him from being there?"

"Make him go somewhere else?" the girl added.

"Brilliant," Sonya yelped, clapping her hands. "You're so close. And how do we do that?"

There was silence as people puzzled over what to say.

"Come on, think about it. Martin you're still at school at the time, right?"

"Yeah."

"And everything's alright there, is it?"

"Yup." I looked across the blank faces to see if anyone else knew what she was getting at.

"But would your Dad know if they weren't?"

"Er. No."

"Unless....." Sonya goaded, letting the words hang for one of us to end the sentence. "Unless...."

"Unless someone told him," said the front row girl, looking really chuffed with her performance.

"Correct. But who?" Sonya pressed. Not Martin, he'd look mental remember. Try this, and this isn't usually the Thompson's way, but what if honesty wasn't the best policy? In this particular case."

"I could phone him," I said, finally piecing things together.

"Yes....." Sonya was beaming again.

"And pretend to be, I don't know, my Head of Year or my English teacher or something."

"Yes....."

"And tell him that I need to meet him, urgently, on Tuesday morning because I'm worried about Martin. About me."

"Excellent. Well done everyone, that's GOLD. Good Objectives Legitimise Decisions," Sonya said, giving me the thumbs up.

"Thanks," I replied.

"Ok then guys," Sonya called. "Quickly before we break for lunch, objective two."

The excited chatter simmered down and I pressed on, conscious of the fact that the group was probably hungry and that I was nearly home. I flipped the next page of the

103

chart to reveal the list of horse racing results I'd Googled the night before and waited for silence.

"The problem is I can get the money, that's fine, but it's in old bank notes and I wouldn't know where to start with setting up a bank account in a time I didn't belong. The room stayed silent.

"Any ideas," Sonya asked as I turned into my street.

"Again thinking outside of the box," she continued. "Martin has got the results of every sporting fixture for the next year. Priceless information but worthless in his current situation."

"He could just stay in 1985 and be a millionaire," chirped the funny guy, but his appeal was wearing thin.

"No. Try again. Come on people. Martin?"

But I just didn't know. My brilliant plan was falling apart at the seams. As I walked along I took the last of the day's race results out of my back pocket. It had taken hours the night before sitting at the computer searching for race meetings, track times and results.

"What a complete waste of time," I thought dejectedly before suddenly being hit by an idea.

"You stupid twat."

I'd spent hours in front of the computer but I'd failed to see what was staring right at me the whole time. It wasn't the horses, or the football or the Boat Race I needed to invest my money in, it was something far more tangible, far more long term and if I played it right, far more profitable.

"Thanks Sonya."

Chapter Ten

It was just after 5pm as I finished my tea and booted-up the computer and by the time I switched-off I was an expert on Apple Inc. The company was founded by friends Steve Jobs and Steve Wozniak on April Fool's Day 1976 and would go on to transform the 21st century with computers, software and the seemingly unstoppable IPod. But in 1985 the firm had not long released its first Apple Macintosh and was an infant compared to the multi-billion dollar company it would become. I knew nothing about shares, where to buy them or from who but if I could take a bite out of Apple, I'd be set for life. The phone rang just as I was mid-way through my Rockefeller-inspired daydream.

"Hello."

"Mart it's me," Linda announced. "Have you been to the grave?"

"Yeah. I was there today."

"Well Auntie Sharon was there this afternoon and she said it's still a right state."

"Yeah, there's still a bit to be done, but I'll get it finished."

"When Mart? The anniversary's on Saturday."

"I know, I've just been-"

"Why aren't you at work? I rang this morning when you didn't answer your phone and they said you were off this week."

"Yeah, I am. I'm taking some time off. So I'll be able to get it done."

"Have you been to see Nan yet?" It was like an

interrogation.

"Not yet. I'm-"

"Everyone's been Mart. All the cousins. She's been asking about you."

"Has she? What did you say?"

"Susan and Wendy were there last night and Sharon said Danny's on his way up from London, and it's his birthday tonight."

"It's probably been his birthday all day," I quipped, trying to lighten her up.

"You're not funny Mart, this is serious. She's not gonna be around forever."

"Ok." She was right. "I'll go down tonight, alright?

"You'd better."

"I will. Look I'd better get going, I'll see you later."

"Ok. And don't forget the grave."

"Yeah. Bye."

Boarding the bus I tried telling myself that I'd had a lot on my plate, with work and time travel and everything but it didn't wash. I was a self-absorbed shit. Yes, I had a lot on, but there was still time to visit my Nan. Actually I had loads of time; I had a time machine, well, time-hole-thingy.

It was the smell that did it first, it always was. So clean, so antiseptic.

"Hi. Can you tell me where the Cancer Ward is please," I asked a friendly looking woman on reception.

"Oncology?"

"Pardon?"

"Do you mean Oncology?" she asked.

"Er. I don't know. My Nan's having chemotherapy."

Linda had told me which ward but I'd not really been listening.

"She's probably on the Vesey Wing. Third Floor. You go right through the double doors, take the first right, then the third left. Ok?"

"Thanks."

I had to ask another two people before I found the right ward. That was the other thing I hated about these places, they were like a rabbit warren. A woman at the nursing station pointed me to my Nan's bed and I approached quietly. I had a feeling I might still make a run for it when I heard my name called.

"Martin." It was my cousin Danny.

"Hello mate, good to see you."

"Yeah you too. I was hoping I'd see you while I was up here."

"Cheers. Linda said you were back, she spoke to your Mom this afternoon."

"Oh, she's telling everyone. How are ya?

"Good thanks. You?"

"Fine, apart from all this. Are you still at Thompson's?"

"Yeah." If I was being vague it was because he was the last person I was telling anything to.

"I heard something on the radio on the way up about a woman getting food poisoning from one of the shops up here. Wasn't your lot was it?"

"Oh fuck off." I thought. It was the way he said 'up here',

107

like you had to get a visa to go to London.

"Dunno. Haven't heard that much about it. Anyway, are you back for long?"

"Just tonight, gotta be back in the morning."

"Yeah?"

"Yeah. My Mum said you haven't been able to get down here much. You got a lot on?" I could never decide if it was sarcasm or sincerity with Danny.

"Yeah, you know, work and everything."

"I know, I've been in Munich all week. This is the first chance I've had to get up here."

"And, your girlfriend is she....?"

"Francesca? No she's in New York all this week. I'm heading out to see her on Friday."

"Wow. So how's Nan?"

"She says she's fine. But I think it's a brave face. She's asleep now."

There are some people you just never think will get old, my Nan was one of them. She looked so small lying there and so tired, nothing like the woman I'd grown up with. And that's why I hated hospitals so much, because if you were there it meant someone you loved was hurt or dying.

"Horrible isn't it, to see her like that?"

"Yeah." Danny sighed. Maybe I was too hard on him, she was his Nan too.

"I told her I'd pay for her to go private but she said she was happy here."

"She's gonna be ok though?" I asked.

"I don't know. It doesn't look good. You smoke for 50 years

and this is where you end up." And she had, even after Grandad died of heart disease. We both stood in silence for a minute. Danny spoke first.

"We'd better leave her in peace." And we crept away nearer to the nursing station. I was just about to make my excuses and leave when he threw me a curve ball.

"You got anything planned for tonight?"

"Err, not sure."

"Well we're just going out for a few drinks later. My Mom and a few old friends. You're welcome to come along."

"Cheers. I'll let you know, I'm a bit-"

"Don't worry it won't be like my 18th, you won't have to dress up as Little Red Riding Hood again," he smiled.

"I wasn't Red Riding Hood," I shot back. "I was Eliot from ET. He wore a red-hooded top when they're on bikes at the end."

"I know, I'm just playing with you. It was a good party though. Singing, dancing, I drank too much and threw up in a plant pot. That fight out the back. Can you believe it was 20 years ago?"

It finally dawned on me.

"It was today wasn't it? Tonight I mean? Your party was 20 years ago?"

"Yeah."

"Of course." I turned, ready to rush out. "Sorry Danny, I've gotta go," I tried to excuse myself, before another curve ball crashed in.

"Martin?" I turned around.

"Rachel?" She was dressed as a nurse.

109

"What are you doing here?"

"My Nan." I nodded towards the bed. I really had to go.

"Mrs Simpson's your Nan? She's a lovely lady."

"Yeah, thanks. Look, sorry but I have to run."

"Oh, ok. I came into your supermarket today. They said-"

"Yeah, I've been off. Sort of. Sorry. Look sorry. I really wish I could chat but I've got to rush-off. And Danny, sorry, I won't be able to make your thing tonight, I've just remembered something."

"Are you alright mate?"

"Yeah, thanks." I turned to Rachel. "Will you be here tomorrow?"

"Yes, from two."

"Great. Danny have a good birthday, it was good to see you again."

"You too. You sure everything's alright?"

"Yeah it's fine. Give my love to Nan. Sorry, but I've got to run."

Chapter Eleven

The fancy dress shop was long closed by the time I got into Sutton, virtually everywhere was. I remembered Danny went as Han Solo, and was pretty sure that was the only reason he wanted a fancy dress party. He was the only child of my Auntie Sharon and Uncle Peter. My Dad used to say they were nouveau riche but I didn't really understand what that meant. It was still bothering me about how I was going to make sure Dad didn't get into that car. I would try Sonya's solution and give him a call from the school, but what if that didn't work? I knew I couldn't just knock on the door with a grim warning about the hazards of motorway driving, but the party was the perfect place to speak to him. Cheers Danny. But before that would be possible, I needed a costume. On the last two visits back I'd worn old jeans and a grey jumper, and no one had raised an eyebrow, it's not as if I'd worn a futuristic silver space suit. But this was fancy dress and a silver space suit would have come in handy. The light was just being switched off at The Hospice Shop when I arrived at the front door looking hot and flustered from running the length of Sutton Parade. The old man said he was only there because he was stocktaking and that I had 15 minutes before his wife came to collect him. It was the light brown tweed jacket that first caught my eye. It was perfect; the patches on the elbows were a bonus. I completed the look with a brown V-neck jumper, a cream shirt and grey trousers. The whole thing came to £17.

"For a fancy dress party." I told the man. "I'm going as a Geography teacher."

"Oh. Hope you have a good time." He frowned slightly.

"I will. And thanks again." I was just about to leave when I had another brainwave.

"Actually, how much is that scarf over there?"

Saturday November 9th 1985

A group of kids on BMXs hung around outside the Odeon. It was a wet and miserable night and apart from the odd reveller the streets were quiet. I was so excited about getting to the party that I sprinted from 'the opening' back into Sutton and as I hurried past the shops and restaurants I almost ran straight past them. It was Jill I spotted first. I only worked with her for a short time but I've always been good with faces, even when they're disguised beneath an 80s hairdo. Dennis looked exactly the same, just a slightly thinner version of the bloke who suspended me two days earlier. They sat in the window of a wine bar called The Stolen Kiss and it was the happiest I think I'd ever seen him. Not counting a short stint at Beckett's Foods, Dennis Johnson had been part of the Thompson's family throughout his career. He joined the firm in the mid-70s and quickly rose through the ranks. The first I heard of him was when Thompson's bought the land next door to my branch for the extension and rumours were immediately rife that Ian Baxter was on his way out. Things changed quickly with Dennis' arrival, the Baxter-era made way for a complete over-haul that most people objected to, at least at first. DJ's staff strategy was to divide and conquer the none-believers by appointing fellow company men into new, previously unheard of and mostly unnecessary positions. If I'm honest I think I've got to say that I was actually quite impressed with him at first. His fight-them-on-the-beaches-style battle-cries at staff meetings were a call to arms against the ensuing Buy-Co invasion, Thompson's closest rivals. But his well-rehearsed speeches quickly wore thin and on his third day, during his first store inspection, he made Sally Adkins cry during an unwarranted outburst about how much make up she was wearing. It was the only time I ever stood-up to Dennis and as I tried to intervene, joking that it was a good thing that staff took pride in their appearance, he sent poor Sally to the staff room to tidy herself up and targeted his tirade towards me. During another public tongue-lashing, he lambasted Nick Shaw for not smiling enough at customers. Nick had been in hospital the day before for x-rays on his nose after being beaten up on the way home from a club; he could barely speak, the poor bloke, let alone smile when he handed over their order. But for those who Dennis liked, life was easy. Pay rise requests went through, holiday time was granted and his daily inspections were nothing more than a friendly chat and a chance to be seen sharing a joke with the boss. I was already running late for the party but standing outside I felt it hard to drag myself away. The sight of a young Dennis smarming by candlelight was almost too much to bear and I considered running in, pouring Jill's Piña colada over his head and legging-it out before he knew what had happened. But watching, as he sipped white wine and stared lovingly across the table, it somehow destroyed the myth of Dennis Johnson. I spent a minute longer to capture the moment before heading-off.

If anyone tells you the buses used to run on time, tell them that they didn't in 1985. It was almost 8pm by the time I reached the pub and I knew I didn't have long. We stayed until the end, I remembered that much. Mom drove Dave and I home, dropping Auntie Shelly off on the way back. Linda stopped out with Danny and his mates and my Dad stayed to help with the clearing up and came back later, that gave me about three hours.

With the night in full swing I was able to slip in unnoticed and made a beeline for the bar.

"Pint of Carling please." I asked the barman, who had entered into the spirit of things and was dressed as a pirate.

"72p please." I could get used to these prices, I thought as I counted out the change and handed it over before turning to face the room. A sense of nervous excitement rose from the pit of my stomach.

"Unbelievable," I muttered into my beer. I was at the same family party for the second time and in the room next door, as far from the speakers as they could get, sat my Mom, Dad and grandparents. The room was a mish-mash of superheroes, screen villains and a robot trying to break dance. The sound of Dead Or Alive's You Spin Me Round was faded out.

"Right then you motley crew I wanna see everybody up here

dancing 'cause it's close to midnight and…this is Thriller…."
A second of dead-air passed before the synthesized chords
kicked in. The DJ stood hovering over two turn-tables
positioned behind a red-blue-yellow-and green light display.
He was dressed as Michael Knight. It was 8.25pm. My
Grandad Stan, my Mom's dad, died when I was 15 and it was
rare for me to think about him, but as he made his way
across the dance floor he was just as I remembered, albeit
dressed as Al Capone. As he approached and stood beside
me, I wish I'd asked him if he wanted a drink but I was too
stunned to move. I tried not to stare as he stood there
waiting to be served, prising a Senior Service cigarette out of
its packet. People danced, the lights flashed and as I watched
my Grandad 18 years after he died, it felt like these weren't
real people, they were ghosts. It wasn't a party, it was a
séance.
"Ha, ha, ha, ha, ha, ha, ha, ha, haaaa." Vincent Price's eerie
laughter faded out and the Knight Rider opened up the mic
again.
"Great to see so many faces here tonight folks. I'll be
slowing things down a bit later on but for now this is a brand
new one… this is Fergal Sharkey."
My Grandad looked really well considering he only had two
years left to live. Fag in one hand, pint in the other, at least
he was out enjoying himself. I could see my Uncle Andrew
on the dance floor, he was dressed as a priest. Elsewhere,
Bruce Lee played the fruit machines, whilst a soldier bought
some crisps. I stayed at the bar and got another drink, too
afraid of who or what I might find if I ventured into the

115

Lounge.

"Like I said, any requests come and let me know. Just mind the wires down the front when you come up, and kids absolutely no touching the lights. Now then, everyone on the dance floor, 'cos this is Dexys Midnight Runners."

The gypsy fiddle intro of Come on Eileen shot out of the speakers and the reaction was instantaneous. Danny appeared in a white shirt and black waistcoat, a homemade blaster at his hip. He was joined by four mates (a boxer, a Roman, a bloke with a Freddie Kruger hand and a woman dressed as a cat) and they bounced around like drunken Irishmen. Others saw the fun and came through (another pirate, two St Trinian's and a bloke with Chris Waddle hair). Linda was dressed as Madonna, she would've been 17. She bound through the door then back into the lounge. I had never considered how old she was looking these days until I saw how young she'd been. She re-emerged dragging a balding James Bond onto the dance floor. He was greeted with a cheer by Danny and his marauding mates. The music wound down to a stop before gearing up again at a fraction of the pace.

"Come on Eileen…."

It was the bit they had all been waiting for and they responded with claps and foot stamps.

"Too-loo rye-aye….."

The next line was faster, then faster still. People were smiling as they jumped and danced. The claps were so fast they became an applause. For a moment it was magic.

"…. I'll hum this tune forever….."

116

The dancing became a frenzy of crazy jigs and loutish stomping. Danny hugged the Roman. A school girl pulled faces at Chris Waddle and an over-weight Adam Ant wore a mile-wide grin as sweat dripped down his face, washing away his eye-liner. Linda and James Bond were exhausted but laughing heartedly. Even in his rented white tuxedo my Dad looked scruffy, his shirt was untucked at one side and what little hair he had was falling forward. Linda willed him to carry on dancing. He looked different, smaller, less robust. I realised I was holding my breath. It was the first time I had seen my Dad since he'd died, and as I stared at him across the room, it was the happiest I'd ever seen him.

"Right, if anyone's got a Ford Cortina parked outside, you've left your lights on," said Michael Knight as he faded the music down just long enough to introduce the next record. "In the meantime ladies, I wanna see those skirts fly off 'cause this is Bucks Fizz, and 'Mind up'".

My dad loosened his black bowtie and caught his breath, his shirt looked too tight across his middle. He stayed on the dance floor as my Auntie Sharon jived towards him in a red ball gown.

"Who are you then?" asked a teenage Lone Ranger, leaning in towards me, stinking of booze.

"Dr Who," I said looking down at the scarf that trailed past my waist.

"Who?" He was really pissed.

"Dr Who."

"Oh. Knock, knock." I'd actually been expecting this.

"Who's there?" I replied.

"You are." And he broke into a fit of laughter. A pretty cowgirl came over to him.

"Joe, Rob's got some vodka, you coming?" she asked and the pair of them staggered off. Then it made sense.

"So you're my alcoholic Uncle Joe?" I muttered into my drink. "Better get used to these bars kid."

Just as he promised, Michael Knight dimmed the lights, wound the music down and Phyllis Nelson's Move Close drew couples to the dance floor. Seizing the opportunity he slipped the headphones over his thick mane, ducked out between the speakers and dashed over to the bar.

"Carling Black Label. Another free one for the DJ?" he asked and the barman obliged. Feeling emboldened by the party and the two pints I'd downed in quick succession, I leant in.

"Knight Rider?" I asked, looking him up and down.

"You what?"

"Knight Rider? You know, 'a shadowy flight into the dangerous world of a man who does not exist.....'"

"What?" he sounded aggressive.

"That's who you've come as, haven't you?"

"No."

"Oh, sorry." I muttered. He looked like he was about to hit me.

"Are you bent or something?"

"No."

"Well you're a dickhead then," he swore as he grabbed his pint and stormed-off.

I stood at the bar for more than an hour and by my third

pint I was no closer to joining the rest of my family.

"Just to let you know the buffet's now open, so save me a sandwich. This was requested by Sandra, it's Art Garfunkel, from Watership Down." I looked on as two of my younger cousins Mandy and Emma (an ice-skater and a hippy), bounced around like bunnies when fate gave me the shove I needed and my Dad came walking over to the bar.

"Pint of Blackthorn, a white wine and a Coke with a straw please," he asked the barman. I assumed the Coke was for me, or Eliot to be more accurate. Looking at him closely for the first time in years my first thoughts were to wonder if we were alike. As he stood there waiting for his order I tried to figure out what bits I'd inherited. He turned to me. I looked away.

"Well if it isn't the old time traveller himself," he said.

"What?"

"You've come as Dr Who?" he looked a bit embarrassed.

"Oh. Yes." I breathed out. "Course I have. Well noticed," I encouraged as I waved my striped scarf and stared at the face that was so familiar.

"So which one are you then?"

"Err." I couldn't concentrate.

"Which incarnation?" He was a bit merry.

Annoyingly I could only think of Sylvester McCoy. "Err, I forget his name, the one with black curly hair."

"Tom Baker."

"Yes, Tom Baker."

"He was great but I always liked Jon Pertwee, the third Doctor."

"Did you?" The conversation wasn't going where I'd expected.

"Oh yeah. I loved it in those days."

"You were a Dr Who fan?" I was fascinated.

"From the very beginning. 1963 I think it was."

"Really? I didn't know that." He frowned slightly. "I mean you don't get many Dr Who fans these days."

"Well I was. Still am I suppose."

"Yeah?"

"Yes, I always enjoyed science fiction." I was talking to my Dad. I was actually having a conversation with my Dad. His voice drawing ripples from my memory. "All the old ones, I suppose, The Day the Earth Stood Still, Quartermass and the Pit."

"Do you still watch them?"

"Not really. I've seen some on video but I don't have the time like I used too. I wanted to watch that Close Encounters of the Third Kind but I haven't seen it yet."

"It came out in 1977."

"Oh well, I'm sure I'll get round to it someday."

A tightness gripped my chest and I took a sharp intake of breath. He looked at me quizzically and turned to check on his order. An overwhelming feeling suddenly made me unsteady on my feet. I wanted to grab his arm, and tell him who I was, who he was to me, and make him promise not to die, not again. I looked over at Danny talking to the DJ.

"What about Star Wars?" I asked, trying to keep the conversation going.

"Oh, I saw them with my lads but they are a bit too, I don't know, silly."

"Silly?"

"Yes. Always liked my science fiction to be heavy on the science. Too many laser battles for my liking."

"The Rebels are trying to bring down the Empire, of course there are laser battles," I pointed out. My breathing returning to normal.

"I know, but I like more realistic films, films that show what it would be like to travel to other planets or deep into the galaxy."

"Yeah?"

"Yes, always have done. I suppose my generation grew up looking at the stars, wondering what it would be like to travel into space."

"Or time?" I asked.

"Yes Doctor, or time."

"So where would you go? I mean when?" It was like a proper pub conversation. Father and son, a few beers, a hypothetical discussion about time travel.

"I don't know. Somewhere in the future, somewhere beyond my years."

"Not the past?"

"Oh, I've travelled to the past."

"What? How?"

"History books. You can travel to anywhere you want to."

"Oh. But, I mean, what if you could really go back."

"Why bother?"

"To see things, to change things."

"There'd be no point."

"No point? Why?"

"Because you can't change the past."

"50 quid in my pocket says you can", I thought.

"But what if you could?" I asked.

"But you can't. You should know that Doctor, the past is the past. It's done, finished."

"Then what's the point in all this if I can't..?"

"No, no. You're forgetting Doctor, the past is where the true power lies. It's in learning about the past that we can make real changes."

"To what?"

"To the future."

"Two pound twenty please," asked the Pirate and my Dad counted out the change and handed it over. He picked up his tray before turning back to me.

"Nice talking to you Doctor."

"You too. By-the-way," I asked. "Which one are you then?"

"Which what?"

"Which Bond?" And I gestured towards his tux.

"Oh, I'm not James Bond."

"No?"

"No, I'm Rick Blaine. Bogart in Casablanca. 'Here's looking at you kid'," he smiled as he walked away.

As the night drew to a close my Mom sat talking to my Auntie Anne, who wasn't wearing any shoes as she'd gone as Sandy Shaw. Linda, still in her head-to-toe Like a Virgin costume, stood doe-eyed chatting to the DJ. My Nan, a 1930s gangster's moll, danced slowly with my Grandad Stan to Always on My Mind. They looked lovely together. A group of young boys, who'd long jettisoned their costumes, were getting told off for sliding on their knees across the wooden floor. I dashed in still wearing my red top and said something to my Dad, he smiled at me and I turned and ran back. I looked tired. It was impossible not to feel sorry for that kid, knowing everything he goes through that week. But not now I was here to stop it. I still didn't know how I was going to do it, just that I would.

"If I take his car then he can't die in a car crash," I thought as I moved towards the doors.

"We're gonna end the night with another slow one. If you've got a party or a wedding coming up you can find me in the Yellow Pages, or the number's on my van. Hope you've had a good one. I definitely have. This is Spandau Ballet. True."

I took one last look at my Dad before leaving. I had to fight the urge to go up to him and tell him: "You're wrong, you can change the future. I will tomorrow and you'll never know how things could have been."

Chapter Twelve

Standing in the toilet cubicle I placed my hand against the back wall for balance. The exhilaration of being back, coupled with five pints and no dinner, had taken its toll. I looked at my watch and had to focus my eyes to read the digital display. It was 10.52pm. The party was winding down, the lights had gone on and the Moms were going around clearing up the tables, placing what was left of the buffet trays in black bin bags for their journey home. I tried to compose my thoughts but the fog of drunkenness got the better of them. I left the cubicle and headed over to the sink and giving the water a minute to run warm, I looked in the mirror. An old, tired face looked back. My skin looked pale under the strip-lighting and the faintest wrinkles were beginning to appear at the edges of my eyes. My hair had begun to recede and the first hints of grey had emerged at my temples. No wonder my Dad didn't recognise me. I closed my eyes for a moment and enjoyed the warm water on my injured hand. I thought about the first time I would have looked in that mirror and seen my 13-year-old self looking back. I opened my eyes and smiled. Yes, I was a supermarket middle manager, I thought, but I was also a time traveller. Hot chicken counter supervisor by day, explorer of the fourth dimension by night.

I left the toilet and turned right through a fire exit propped opened by a bar stall to allow access to the car park at the back. I stepped out into the night and inhaled deeply, the cold air bringing a sense of clarity I'd failed to find in the gents. I gazed up at the clear, starry night sky and looked forward to seeing the stars in an hour's time when they were 20 years older. I took one last look over my shoulder, reluctant to leave. Back in the pub, kids were being rounded-up, family members were saying their goodbyes and the last of the tables were being cleared away as the bar staff urged people to finish their glasses. I took three steps across the car park and stopped. What I heard was more of a squeak than a scream, then a pleading voice. If it had been unfamiliar, I'm not proud to say, I probably would have carried on walking. I stood and listened, trying to hear through the last of the chaos still reverberating around the function room. Just audible was the faintest sound of feet shuffling against the gravel and I looked over towards a dark blue van in the dimly lit corner of the car park. It was facing me, its back doors were open but the lights were off.

Another shuffle of feet and this time hushed voices. Quietly, I stepped back towards the pub and the van's white lettering came into view: Shaun Byford Mobile Disco 021 351 1219. I inched closer, not sure what I would see, not sure if it was any of my business.

"Get off Shaun", Linda cried out.

"Aw, come on", The Knight Rider replied impatiently. "Don't be a prick tease."

I dashed over and saw Linda sitting on the back of the open van. Shaun Byford standing over her, his hands underneath her skirt, gripping her thighs as she tried to squirm away. She looked frightened and drunk.

126

"The fuck do you want?" Byford spat towards me as I reached the corner of his van.

"Get inside, now!" I told Linda and she jumped up.

"Who the fucking hell do you think you are?" he snarled.

"Get inside," I ordered again, raising my voice. She looked at me, then at Byford.

"You need to fuck off mate before I kick your fucking head in," he warned, his face now enraged.

I wish I could say that Linda ran inside, that Byford turned and squared-up to me. That I told him I didn't want any trouble but he threw a right-hook which I blocked with my left forearm. I wish I could say that I stepped towards him and at close-quarters I raised a knee to his groin, followed by an uppercut to his chin that sent him flying backwards and onto the floor, his eyes watering and his hands cut by glass and gravel. I wish I could say that I told him not to mess with people's sisters and walked away to the sound of his sniffs and sobs.

But that didn't happen. He lunged at me and I threw my arms up in front of my face. He unleashed a hard jab which connected with my forehead, knocking me off balance. A second blow struck me on the left ear causing an immediate stinging sensation and a shooting pain down my neck. His third strike crashed into my bottom lip, filling my mouth with blood. As the blows rained down it didn't cross my mind to hit back, I suppose I just wasn't programmed that way. Instead, I thought about Ken Edmunds, my predecessor's predecessor on the Oven Counter. Ken was the longest serving supervisor in the whole store when I joined Thompson's in 1990. He was a kind man with a big laugh and an understanding manner. I approached him early during my shift two weeks before to try and book off Friday 12 November 1999. Rather than tell him the truth, I told him I was going to a wedding in Stoke. Ken said it was fine and that I could either book it as holiday or swap with one of the other full-time members of staff. Rather than going through the hassle of finding someone to swap with I went to HR with a holiday request form signed by Ken and booked a day's leave. When I saw him next he greeted me with a smile and asked how the wedding had gone and I invented an elaborate tale about how it was two old Uni mates who I didn't really see that often but that it was nice to have been invited. He then told me about his daughter's wedding and we had a good chat about his honeymoon in 1968. Unbeknown to Ken, I wasn't throwing confetti at my non-existent undergraduate pals in the Potteries, I was in the cinema at 11am watching Fight Club on the day of its release. Having read the book years earlier and having been a fan of David Fincher since Aliens 3, I couldn't wait to see Fight Club on the big screen. It had been the second film I'd booked the day off to see that year, having invented a reason to be off work the day Star Wars Episode One: The Phantom Menace had disappointed us all that summer. Watching the bone-crunching violence, the slick editing and Brad Pitt's vintage leather jackets, I was a world away from my life of servitude at Thompson's.

"I want you to hit me as hard as you can," Tyler Durden tells his Edward Norton-looking alter ego. They scrap, they chat, they start a club for the Generation X-ers, not given the dignity of a depression to survive or a war to fight. They plan a revolution, spreading their ideas with Invasion of the Body Snatchers-style ease. They provoke, they torment, they blackmail. They wear tuxedos and scars and chisel their bodies down to anatomical efficiency. They sound a call-to-arms to men raised by women, to men fighting a 'spiritual war' against themselves. And I heard every word.

"How much can you really know about yourself if you've never been in a fight?" Tyler asks.

"Not much," I answered from the third row of an Erdington multi-plex. Fight Club spoke to me in a way no film had done since watching Raiders of the Lost Ark at my Nan's house on Christmas day in 1986. There I was on screen, a Space Monkey ready to act, a man ready to fight, no longer willing to squander my youth or talent or potential.

As I fell to the car park floor and Byford kicked me hard in the ribs I thought of Tyler and Ken Edmunds and The Phantom Menace. I wondered if being beaten-up counted as a fight, then I remembered Tyler's first homework assignment.

"I want you to start a fight. And lose," he tells his congregation of fired-up white collar hooligans, as they stand in a basement without shirts and shoes. I remembered Tyler being beaten up for the greater good, how he laughs as his bloodied face is thumped into the concrete floor and realised I wasn't losing the fight - every blow I took was a victory.

"Not so fucking cocky now are ya?" Byford mocked, the tip of his leather slip-on shoe connecting with my side.

Linda dived on his back and halted the kicks.

"Get off me you bitch," he screamed, turning as he landed a backhanded slap across her cheek.

Byford kicked me again. The landlord of the pub came running out, a heavy-set man in his late-50s. He shoved Byford against the wall and told Linda to get inside.

"He started it," Byford protested. "He's a poof, he was coming onto me earlier".

The landlord picked me up off the floor.

"You alright mate?" he asked.

"Yeah", I replied and as much as my body hurt, I *was* alright.

"You'd better get on home then," he added.

I took a moment and exhaled deeply.

"Shaun is it?" I asked.

"Yeah," Byford sneered.

"Thanks," I said, before falling unconscious to the floor.

Sunday November 10th 1985

I awoke in a hospital bed. I was in a small room, just off the main ward lit only by a streetlight outside of the window. A drip was attached to my left hand and I was propped-up by three pillows. My face felt swollen. I turned towards the door and sitting in a high-backed chair was my Dad.

"You're here?" I said. "What are you doing here?"

"I came with you in the ambulance. How are you feeling?"

"I'm ok. Sore. What happened?"

"I don't know. The landlord found you lying in the car park. You must have hit your head, it was bleeding quite badly.

Too much to drink?"

"Something like that." If Linda hadn't told him, I wasn't going to.

"He said you were spark-out. He tried to find who you were with but nobody knew?"

"I told you earlier, I'm a time traveller."

He smiled.

"Thanks for coming with me."

"That's alright. I've got lads of my own, I suppose I like to think somebody would do the same for them one day."

"They will," I reassured him.

"So what's your name? Where are you from?"

I was too tired for any more lies. "My name's Martin. I used to be from around here but I haven't been back in a long time."

"I've got a lad called Martin."

"Yeah, I saw him at the party, the one in the red top?"

"That's him. So who were you there with?"

"No one. I just wandered in to get out of the rain. The music was good so I stayed."

"You said you were Dr Who."

"I'm a geography teacher, the tweed goes with the job."

He laughed loudly before realising where he was. We both stayed silent for a moment.

"Is there anyone I can contact for you?" he asked.

"No thanks. It's late. I'll sort things out in the morning."

"So are you married? Kids?"

"No, neither."

He looked surprised.

"It's not that uncommon where I'm from."

"And where's that?"

"Erdington."

He smiled again.

"I'm glad to see you're looking better, you had me worried in the ambulance."

"Oh?"

"You don't remember? You woke up, took one look at me and leapt up like you'd seen the Ghost of Christmas Past. You kept screaming that it was your anniversary and we were going to crash. He had to give you something to settle you down."

I looked at him in the low light. The curtain by the wall cast a shadow across his face. The top two buttons of his dress-shirt were undone and there were three spots of blood on his sleeve. His hair was heavily receding and his eyes looked watery. His glasses had slipped down his nose, like they did when he read the paper in his armchair.

"Thanks for this. Thanks for everything," I told him. A tear welled-up in my eye and rolled down my right cheek.

"That's alright son." He touched my right arm and gave it a faint squeeze. "I'm just glad you're ok." I held his gaze and for a moment I thought he recognised me.

"Oh, before I forget," he said. "Your clothes and shoes are in the cupboard there. They had to cut your shirt off, it had a lot of blood on it. They put your wallet and your pager in a bag. I put them under your trousers for safekeeping."

I nodded. He smiled back.

"Well then, I'd better be off. It's late and you need some rest."

"Thanks for sitting with me."

"That's alright. I usually hate these places. It's the smell, brings back too many memories."

He leant forward to get up.

"Wait. I need to tell you something."

He froze in his position, looking on with concern.

"It'll sound crazy but please, you have to wait until I've finished. What I was saying in the ambulance-"

The door opened and a stout looking Matron shot my dad a severe look.

"I told you ten more minutes an hour ago," she hissed, her voice low but stern.

"Right, yes. Sorry," my Dad replied sheepishly as he stood up.

"Wait!" I called out.

"No, say your goodbyes and come with me please," she ordered, placing a hand on my Dad's arm.

"Please. Just a minute I-"

"Quiet," she barked. "You'll wake the whole ward. He can come back tomorrow."

"I can if you like," my Dad interjected.

"Please I just need to-"

"Enough."

She turned my Dad towards her and led him out. The door slowly closed and I heard their footsteps disappearing down the hall.

"Wait!" I cried out again, sitting up in the bed. A sharp pain caused my head to spin. My feet found the floor but I felt too weak to stand. The drunkenness that had insulated me from the worst of Byford's beating had gone and the painkillers I'd been administered in the ambulance were wearing off. I sat on the edge of the bed, looking out of the window. My head began to clear but I knew it was too late. I touched my lip before raising my fingers to my cheek. Staring out across the empty car park I was hit by the severity of what had happened. In trying to save Linda, I could have been killed. What if I had died, here in 1985? What if I'd cracked my skull open or the bleeding had been worse? What would have happened to me, to my body? Would I have been laid out on a mortuary slab while they tried to find a next-of-kin? What then? Buried? Incinerated? What about my things, my wallet, my mobile? Who would have found it? What would they have done with it? A flip phone, digital camera, memory card; all 20 years too early. It could have changed everything, altered life as I knew it. And what about me in the future? Or the lack of me. The last time anyone saw me I was acting strange, racing out of the hospital, the same one I'm in now, never to be seen again. Perhaps the man in the charity shop would recognise my description on Central News and call the police. Who would report me missing? Linda probably when I failed to show-up at Dad's anniversary. She'd give them a statement and a recent picture. The police would sit on it for a few days, waiting for me to resurface before launching a more thorough investigation. They would break into my flat and find thousands of pounds in old banknotes. They would go to my work and interview my colleagues. Dennis would tell them about Elaine Baker and the salmonella and that I'd been suspended. He'd tell them something like how bad I was at dealing with stress and that I'd probably offed myself to avoid the shame. With no other lines of enquiry that would become the official verdict.

"Fuck," I said out loud. "I need to get back to the present." I pulled at the cannula in my hand and drew the needle out from my vein. I stood up and found my clothes in the cupboard. I threw my tweed jacket over my gown, pulled my trousers on and gathered my things. Creeping across the ward I managed to make it past the nursing station without being seen and out into the corridor. It was still dark when I got outside and I skulked across the grounds, making sure I wasn't spotted. It took more than an hour to make it back to the flat. With my clothes still on, I fell onto the bed. I lay there for a moment before closing my eyes and for the second time in six hours I passed out.

Chapter Thirteen
Thursday November 10th 2005

I woke up, rolled over and wished I was still asleep. My ribs were bruised and my face still felt swollen. It was ten in the evening and I propped myself up in bed to watch some Sunday night telly. Flicking through the channels I found a much-hated old classic on Film Four, The Seventh Seal. I'd seen it at University but I'd been too angry to watch, betrayed by my 'mate' and broken hearted for the first time. My academic career started badly and went downhill from there. I didn't know what I wanted to do when I finished school. I got quite into books and poetry in Sixth Form and liked the idea of travelling and writing about my experiences like Albert Camus or Jack Kerouac, but Dave told me I needed to get with the real world and get a job. I'd taken English, Geography and Sociology at A-Level but after spending more time at the cinema than attending lessons in my second year the predicted grades weren't good. During a careers day in the school assembly hall I was almost talked into joining the local council as a trainee planning officer and quite liked the idea of being responsible for new buildings but changed my mind when my mate Matt said it sounded shit. The truth was I didn't know what I wanted to do, so in the absence of direction I followed my Mom's advice and reluctantly sent-off my hand-written PCAS application form. I had four rejections but was offered a conditional place to do a geography degree at Darlington Tech. In 1992 it would become the University of the North East but luckily for me it was still a polytechnic and would let you in with three Ds. The weekend before I left home the hardest part was knowing what videos to take, how could I possibly know what films I would want to watch between now and Christmas, I thought?

Craig had said he would drive me up there but his car failed its MOT the week before so I had to borrow money of my Mom and catch the train.

With my scaled-back consignment of worldly goods squeezed into two suitcases and my old school bag I caught the bus into Town and made my way through the crowds to New Street Station. The train journey took forever, passing through towns and cities I'd heard of but never visited. As I left the Midlands, heading further North the feeling of entering a strange No-Man's Land took over my thoughts. I was a Brummie, born and bred and I'd never lived anywhere else. What if they couldn't understand my accent? That nasally twang that was derided by everyone from Auf Wiedersehan, Pet to Red Dwarf. What if I was mocked, laughed at, the butt of the joke? What if my clothes were wrong, my hair, my taste in music? The train passed through Wakefield and I felt my despair worsen. I wasn't cool, I wasn't tough, I wasn't good looking or good at football. These are the things you're meant to be. My stomach knotted more tightly than I'd ever felt and I bit my thumb nail down until it bled.

"Oh fuck," I thought as I stepped off the train at Darlington station. "What am I doing?"

As I struggled to follow the directions I'd been sent to my accommodation, I wished I was still in Sutton, surrounded by the people I'd grown up with. I wished I worked at the Council, attending meetings, compiling reports, bringing the occasional cup of tea and all that stuff the woman at the Careers Fair had promised. I imagined myself getting the train to work, marching to my office in a shirt and tie with all the other commuters. I imagined sitting at my desk in the Council House, unrolling diagrams of new building projects and playing a part in the changing face of Brum. I'd fucked up. A hollow feeling grew. I felt sick and scared and reckless and stupid. I felt lost and alone and it was all my fault. Up until then I'd led a life without consequence. It hadn't mattered if I'd got it wrong because stuff was usually ok, but not this.

I stopped under a streetlight to make-out the last page of directions. Somewhere nearby a dog barked and a man shouted. I stumbled along carrying my heavy suitcases, regretting bringing so many films. I was staying in a shared house a mile from the Poly. A letter I'd been sent said the Halls of Residents would be closed until February because asbestos had been found in the toilets but that 'suitable temporary local accommodation would be provided'.

As I stood outside my new home, a run-down terrace at the edge of a patch of waste ground, I began to cry. Small tears at first, then sobs of despair. A light came on in the downstairs front room and I pulled myself together. I picked up my suitcases and climbed the steps to the front door. Reaching into my jeans for my key, a stereo started up in the

139

front room and loud rave music boomed out. Inside I found my room and without even attempting to meet my housemates, I lay on my bed and cried myself to sleep.

I shared the house with Matt and Dave, two history students from Wendsleydale; Claire from Wigan who we never saw; Clive, a second-year science student from Bristol; Jon, a second year English student from Nottingham; and Emma, a first year drama student from London. As the last to arrive, I had the smallest room up on the third floor. It was a state. The wooden-framed window didn't meet at one side and the cold wind that blew through cancelled out the benefit of the electric heater plugged in next to the door. The room contained a single bed, a wardrobe, a small black and white telly and a chest-of-drawers. I had planned to write a strongly-worded letter because all accommodation was supposed to come with a desk but there was no way one would fit in this room. The wood-chip wallpaper was ripped and there was a dent in the back of the door, presumably from the fist of an equally dissatisfied previous tenant.

As an undergraduate of a Bachelor of Science in Geography, my week consisted of five lectures and two seminars every fortnight. Too afraid to ask what a seminar was during induction week I went along with high hopes, only to discover it involved talking about the things we'd already been taught earlier in the week. I had lectures in Human Geography, Physical Geography, Contemporary Urban Geography, Laboratory Geography and Database Analysis.

140

In addition we had elective modules in either Cartography Design or European Topography and a tutorial session every third Thursday.

The campus was large and busy and because classes were attended by a range of Geography, Science, Maths and Engineering students, you never seemed to see the same people twice. I had heard a lot about the great times I'd have at Uni and the great mates I'd meet, but where were they? My housemates were either at home listening to loud rave music or out with their other friends. I even considered taking up smoking in the hope of meeting people in the canteen under the pretext of needing a light. I'd hoped salvation would come with the chance discovery of the Student Union Film Society poster in the men's toilets. They met once a week to watch and discuss everything from 'classic films to new releases'. I was over the moon. On the day of the first Film Soc meeting I could hardly concentrate as Dr Fitzgerald outlined details of our Earth and Ecological Systems essay. What would they be like? What should I wear? Did I have to bring any films? What if there were girls there? I was too excited to care about applied micro-meteorology, this was the chance I'd been waiting for.

"Hi, I'm here for the Film Soc," I said to a girl with green hair waiting by the door of Student Common Room 3.
"What?"
"The Film Soc," I replied. "I saw a poster….."
"They got the times wrong."
"Sorry?"

"They got the times wrong. Room's booked until 7.30pm."

"Oh, will it be on after that?"

"Dunno," she said in reply.

I stood there for a few moments trying to think of what to say.

"So, do you go to Film Soc?" I asked.

"No."

"Oh. So what are you here for?"

"Waiting for my boyfriend."

I smiled and took a few steps over to the notice board to kill time. Twelve minutes passed until more people arrived.

"You here for the Film Society?" asked a friendly looking man with a Midland accent and a red backpack.

"Yes."

"Is this your first time?"

"Yes."

"Mine too. I'm Gary," he said thrusting out his hand.

"I'm Martin," I replied, unsure how firmly to shake it back.

"Hiya Martin. What you studying?"

"Geography. How about you?"

"Biology. We might have the same classes. Do you have Andy Mason on Thursday mornings?"

"Yeah!" I was getting excited.

"Me too. We should meet up afterwards, get a pint." This sounded great.

"Yeah. Definitely."

"Excuse me. You are here for the Film Society?" asked a heavily accented voice.

Gary and I turned to see a tall girl with brown eyes, curly dark hair and a wide mouth.

"Yes we are," we both replied.

The seats were arranged in a circle from the previous group and Thomas, the Film Society President, apologised and said we'd leave them like that for today but that he'd arrange for them to be in rows for next week's screening. He suggested, as there were a lot of new faces, that we all introduce ourselves, say where we are from and what our favourite film is.

"I'll start. Well guys, welcome to Film Club. I'm Thomas. I'm from Guildford and my favourite film is Saturday Night, Sunday Morning." Shit, I thought. Very worthy.

"I'm Kristen from Bristol and my favourite film is The Third Man." Another good one.

"Hi, I'm Alice and I'm from Northamptonshire. My favourite film is anything by Alfred Hitchcock." Northamptonshire? Hitchcock? Surely you can't be that vague, I thought but Thomas had no such reservations and he gestured towards the next person.

"Hi there, I'm Rob, I'm a Sagittarius and I like Hammer Horror films, fine wine and walks in the country." People laughed. I forced a smile.

"And where are you from?" Thomas asked.

"Oh yeah. I'm from Sunny Manchester."

I was four people away from my introduction. Shit. What should I say? If the truth be told I didn't have a favourite film, I loved loads of them. I hated this stuff, it was like a band fact-file in Just Seventeen.

"Hello, I'm Laura, I'm from Tamworth and my favourite film is Pretty Woman." You can't have that, I thought, it was only released this summer. There should be a rule that the films are at least two years old or something.

"Hi. My name's Peter, I'm from Graz in Austria and my favourite film is probably Local Hero." A strangely Scottish choice for an Austrian. I wondered if he was a Schwarzenegger fan. Anyway. Shit. Think, think, think. Should I go honest or impressive? Commercial or Art House? What about a documentary? Right, it was either Empire Strikes Back or Godard's Vivri Sa Vie. Fuck. I couldn't think.

"Evening. My name's Grant but most people call me Spud. I'm from North London. Favourite film's gotta be Godard's Bande à part." Son of a bitch stole my idea. I couldn't say Vivri Sa Vie now, and I'd read a feature about it in Sight and Sound that summer. Fuck. Ok. Change of plan.

"Hi guys, my name's Jules, I'm from Oslo and my favourite film is Fist Full of Dollars."

Thomas nodded before turning to me.

"Hi, I'm Martin, I'm from Sutton Coldfield and my favourite film is Fritz Lang's M."

I looked around the room and saw the right level of approval and confusion. Perfect. I breathed a sigh of relief. It came to me like a thunderbolt. M. The perfect choice. A taut, black and white thriller. The swansong of German expressionism. The film Lang himself considered his finest piece of work. A masterstroke by him, and now by me.

"I'm Mark, I'm from Portsmouth and my favourite film is The Exorcist." Good choice, I thought, feeling more relaxed. Then the moment I'd been waiting for, the French girl who'd approached us outside.

"Hi, my name is Françoise and I'm from Aubervilliers, near Paris and my favourite film is Star Wars."

Fuck. Fuck. Fuck. Fuck. Fuck, I screamed to myself.

"Hi I'm Sharon from Cambridge and my favourite film is either Blithe Spirit or The Seventh Seal."

You can't allow that Thomas, I fumed. What's the point of rules? I didn't say Battleship Potemkin or Howard the Duck. Make her say just one, I willed.

"Hi, my name's Gary and I'm from Coventry. If I'm totally honest my favourite film is Star Wars as well but as we've had that already I'll say Empire Strikes Back."

The rest of the night was spent discussing our choices and talking about the types of films we wanted to screen during the sessions. Thomas asked me if I had a copy of M I could show but I'd only seen it once on Channel Four when I was babysitting my cousin and hadn't taped it.

"Yeah, I've got it but most of my films are at home," I explained. "I can bring it back after Christmas," I suggested, giving me enough time to buy and re-watch it before then.

As the weeks went by, Film Club became the highlight of my University life, of life in general, and I'd count down the days until the next get together.

I quickly, predictably became infatuated by Françoise and as much as I enjoyed the weekly film chats, it was seeing her that I looked forward to the most. The first proper

145

conversation I had with her was about Dances with Wolves, the second was about the Channel Tunnel. She was 19 and wore leggings and long baggy jumpers with holes in the sleeves that she put her thumbs through. She always had her personal stereo headphones around her neck, although I don't ever remember seeing her listening to music. She smoked Camel Lights and drank a lot of coffee. She was studying English and Philosophy but could also speak Arabic as her grandfather was from Algiers. In the two months I knew her the nearest I got to asking her out was when I said I wanted to watch Flatliners and she said she did too. But instead of taking the initiative and setting a date I bottled it and the next day Gary asked her to a gig.

Looking back, a lot of things weren't going well at the time. I was homesick, discovered drinking, was not attending lectures and missed deadlines - but all I thought I needed was the love of a good woman; a chain-smoking, pouting, REM-loving woman. The first time I saw them together was out one Friday night. Darlington had two nightclubs, Chasers and New York, New York. I ended up in Chasers after drinking with a few people from Chess Club and spotted Gary and Françoise dancing to Take My Breath Away by Berlin. I loved that song and had the Top Gun soundtrack on LP. I wanted nothing more than to kiss her to that song. But Gary had got there first. Drunk, tired and upset I headed home. Thankfully my rowdy housemates were out. Probably standing in a field on happy pills, listening to Kenny Ken, or some other DJ on the flyers posted-up in the downstairs toilet. I helped myself to some whiskey from Clive's cupboard and sat in the living room with the lights off. I'm not sure why I picked up the phone. It might have been drunken indulgence or genuine desperation. I knew the number to my Dad's old office off by heart and knew that his partner Derek Wilson was a technophobe. I dialled the number and it took a moment to connect. I hadn't done this for a year or so and held my breath in case Derek had learned how to record a new message. It rang four times before I heard the sound of a click and a second of recorded background noise.

"Hello, this is Wilson and Brownlow Insurance Brokers," the familiar voice started. I breathed out. "We're not here to take your call at the moment but if you leave your name, number and a short message we will return your call as soon as possible." Then there was a beep.

I hung up and dialled again.

"Hello, this is Wilson and Brownlow Insurance Brokers. We're not here to take your call right now but if you leave your name, number...."

It was the way my Dad said hello that I liked the most, as if I'd just got home from school or come downstairs on a Saturday morning. The room span and I forced myself to try and picture his face but I couldn't. I dialled again.

"Hello, this is Wilson and Brownlow...."

And again.

"Hello...."

I dialled the number 47 times that night, I know that because it showed up on our itemised bill at the end of the quarter. When I heard one of my flatmates at the door I ran upstairs to my room and closed the door behind me. Apart from the occasional visit to the kitchen or bathroom, I stayed in there for the rest of the weekend, and half of the following week. I went back to Birmingham for Reading Week in the middle of November and didn't go back to university again. My personal tutor sent me a letter saying my place would be withdrawn unless I contacted him, but I never did. In mid-January, Craig drove me back up to collect the last of my things and I started at Thompson's soon after I was back. As The Seventh Seal reached its sombre conclusion I took two Paracetamol and got back into bed. I thought about Gary and Françoise and wondered if they were still together. I thought about my Top Gun LP and regretted smashing it up that dark weekend in Darlington. I hoped they were still together. I imagined Gary had moved to France after they graduated and they were now running a vineyard somewhere, surrounded by beautiful dark haired children. I wondered if they ever thought of me, that strange bloke who dropped out of Uni in the first semester, who's now a time-traveller.

Chapter Fourteen

Friday November 11th 2005

It was early the next day. The phone rang.

"What are you playing at Mart?" I didn't say anything. "I knew I couldn't leave it to you. I bloody knew it."

"Linda I-"

"Don't. I don't wanna hear it." Why did you phone me then, I thought?

"I'm sorry, I've really had a lot on." I gingerly touched my thick lip.

"What Mart? What have you had on?"

"I can't really-"

"Have you been sacked? Why haven't you been at work? Is something going on?"

The way I looked at it was, when I changed the past my Dad never dies therefore I wouldn't have to do the grave, so this conversation never actually takes place. It really didn't matter what I said so I may as well take the easy way out.

"I suppose. It's just with the anniversary and everything." It was what they were all expecting to hear anyway. I deliberately paused a second before carrying on: "I suppose it's just brought back a lot of memories."

"Oh Mart why didn't you say?"

"You know….. It's just…. Look, I'm really sorry. I'll get it done today. I promise."

"You don't have to I'll…."

"It's fine.

"As long as you're sure."

"Honestly Linda. I've got it all figured out. I'll fix it, I'll fix everything."

I put the phone down and sighed. I didn't like lying to Linda, but I couldn't exactly tell her the truth. She sounded tired, defeated. I thought back to the energetic teenager who'd spent the whole evening on the dance floor the night before. She'd aged so much since then. And it wasn't just the lines that edged her eyes and mouth; it was the disappointment that seemed to frame her face and tinge her voice. Was it just the years that had changed her, or was it what had happened since? Losing her Dad, getting pregnant while she was still young, marrying a man who seemed to regularly disappoint her. Well if I hadn't had been there last night, I thought, something terrible might have happened to change her even more. Hang on a second. If I'd changed the past last night and prevented Byford from giving her anything more than a sore cheek, she should be different now because of that change. I thought about the conversation I'd just had; she didn't seem any different. I tried to remember back to the night of the party, straining my memory for any evidence of what would have happened, but nothing. Years later Auntie Sharon said something about a fight that night but I presumed it was one of Danny's mates. Had I changed things? I needed to know. I picked up the phone and rang Linda back.

"Hello, it's me."

"Yeah."

"Yeah, I just wanted to say sorry. For this week and

everything." She didn't reply. "I know I can be useless at times but I'm working to try and change things."

"Ok," she replied.

"Yeah. We should see each other more. And the girls and Craig. I do care about you all, you know?"

"Aww Mart, 'couse I do."

"I mean it. Once the anniversary's out the way you should come over, bring the girls, I'll rent Finding Nemo or something and put it on the projector, we'll get popcorn, have a film night. What do ya think?"

"That sounds nice," she said, sounding slightly resigned.

"Great, let's do that then."

"Ok."

"Erm, Linda. Can I ask you something?

"Yeah."

"It's a weird one, but do you remember cousin Danny's party, years ago? His 18th?"

"Yeah."

"Do you remember a fight at the end after we'd gone?"

"Have you been talking to Mom?"

"No. Danny mentioned his party at the hospital the other night. Was there an ambulance or something?"

"A bloke got beaten up, I don't know who he was."

"You didn't see anything?"

"Mart, what is this?" Her voice had changed.

"Nothing. Just asking."

"Well that's all I remember," she snapped, closing the conversation.

"Ok."

"Look I need to get off."

"Ok, sorry. I'll speak to you later."

"Ok, bye," she said before hanging up.

I put the phone down, a dull sense of regret distracting me from the pain in my body. I shouldn't have mentioned that night to Linda. If I had changed things last night, she wouldn't know any different now, and it seemed like all I'd managed to do was piss her off. Oh well, I thought, today I'm going to change everything so none of this will matter. I hurriedly finished my breakfast, my mind firmly fixed. It would have to run like clockwork. I'd lost time but I was certain I could still pull it off, still fulfil both parts of my plan. I'd go back and be at the bookies for first thing and have another five grand by lunch. I'd then phone about the shares before ringing my Dad to arrange an urgent appointment at school the following day. With everything in place, I'd head home to a new 2005, one where my dad was still alive and we go to sci-fi conventions together at weekends. God, a person could go crazy thinking about this. I showered, changed into a black t-shirt, put on my tweed jacket and walked down to the bus stop.

"You can't change the past," he'd said, but I knew I could.

"You can't alter history." But I would prove him wrong.

I waited for the bus, still thinking it through. I have changed things. Parallel Universes or whatever, there was a time, a 1985, when I wasn't standing in betting shops with a list of the names of every winning horse. I didn't go back until 2005 so until then there was a history when I wasn't there and if nothing else the till receipts at the bookies would have looked different without my winnings being paid out. If I could change those then I could change the accident. I boarded the bus and found my usual seat upstairs, right side, three seats from the front. I slouched into a comfortable position and rubbed my hands together, it was a freezing cold morning.

Monday November 11th 1985

I hardly even pretended to listen as the race results came in. As I walked to the counter to collect my winnings my mind was like a tube map as I tried to connect the possibilities and anticipate the history of things to come. When I save my Dad everything will be different. The thought scared me. I wondered what it will be like, will we be close? Where will he and Mom live? Where do I live? Am I in the same flat? Am I married? Kids? Change one thing, change everything. Who knows? If a butterfly can cause a hurricane then what will this do? It all boiled down to cause and effect, but what would be the effects? I thought about it for a long time. "Fuck it. Whatever happens, it'll be worth it."

I inserted two coins and dialled the number I'd just been given by directory enquiries. The line rang twice before the call was connected.

"Good morning. Moore, Spencer and Wright, how may I help you?"

"Err, yes. Hello, I wonder if I can make an appointment with a stockbroker please."

153

"Certainly sir. Are you an existing client?"

"No, first time."

"When were you hoping for?" I put another 5p into the phone.

"I know it's short notice, but tomorrow if possible."

"One moment please." The line went silent. Moore, Spencer and Wright, was a bonds and share trading company founded in 1923 and still going strong in 2005.

"Mr Newton is available between two thirty and three."

"That's great."

"And what name is it please?"

"Martin Brownlow."

"Thank you. And Mr Brownlow for our records, although you are not obliged to say at this stage, what areas are you considering investing in?"

"Computers, mostly, and telecommunications."

"Any particular companies at this stage? And again, you do not have to specify."

"No, it's ok. Microsoft, IBM, Apple, Sony, British Telecom, Nokia and Eriksson. Oh and Golden Wonder." Pot Noodles had yet to make an impact on the British snack buying public.

"One moment please." Again no Vivaldi as I waited. "Ok then sir, two thirty with Mr Newton tomorrow afternoon."

"Thanks very much."

"You're welcome, goodbye." The line went dead and I hung up. Tomorrow afternoon I was going to London. A bus drove past and sent a rush of cold air through the phone box. I pulled out some more change and more nervously

154

than I had expected, I phoned my Dad's office.

"Good morning, Wilson and Brownlow, how can I help you?"

"Hello can I speak to George Brownlow please?"

"Certainly, may I ask who's calling?"

"Yes it's Malcolm Garland." I had no idea what Mr Garland's first name was but neither would my Dad.

"Good morning George Brownlow, how can I help?" Instinctively I lowered my voice.

"Good morning, my name is Malcolm Garland from Sutton Comprehensive. I'm Martin's head of year."

"Is everything alright?" he interrupted.

"Yes, everything's fine. I was just hoping to speak to you about Martin. He doesn't seem to be quite himself lately."

"In what way?"

"Well it's difficult to pin-point but I've spoken to a few other teachers and they are also a little concerned. If you don't mind me asking, is everything alright at home?"

"Well yes. I think so. I-" I cut him short to inject a little urgency.

"Would it be possible to meet with you and your wife in person? I think it would be a good idea."

"Yes of course," he replied with concern. "When should we come in?"

"Well the sooner the better usually with this sort of thing."

"I'm free this afternoon."

"Err. Not too good for me I'm afraid. I'm up to my eyes in coursework at the moment. GCSEs, O Levels, HSCs, it's a very busy time. Um. Tomorrow morning is the earliest I can

155

do. Let's say 9.15am."

For a second it sounded like he was going to agree. I imagined him checking his diary or realising what date tomorrow would be.

"I'm sorry, I can't make it tomorrow morning. Any other time is fine but I have a prior appointment and I really can't rearrange it."

"I'm afraid tomorrow really would be best for me Mr Brownlow, otherwise, with the mock exams-"

"It's just not possible, I'm sorry. I can do any other time. An evening perhaps if that's more convenient for you." I really should have left it at that, he sounded genuinely unable to make it but I pushed it further.

"Mr Brownlow, I think Martin is being bullied."

"Bullied? Bullied by who?"

"Err. We don't know at this stage but erm...."

"Look, I can come down this afternoon. I'll speak to Martin." He sounded worried.

"No, no," I interjected. "No I think it's best if.... Best if I speak to his form teacher and see if he can have a word with him. I think they get on pretty well. And. Err. I'll call you maybe next week and we'll set up some kind of a meeting."

"But I'd really like to get this sorted out straight away, if he's being bullied-"

"Well. At this stage we don't know. It really could be anything. You know what teenagers are like. It's probably a girl or an argument about football," I said desperately trying to withdraw the urgency.

"Yes, it could be, but it could also be that he's being bullied."

156

He started to sound impatient.

"I'm pretty sure he's not being bullied by anyone in particular. Look if you give me a couple of days."

"I'll speak to him tonight."

"No. Err. Probably best if, err, at this stage you don't say anything. He could close up altogether and ....." I had no idea what I was saying so I cut myself short. "Best just to see how things go. We'll handle things this end and erm….."

"Ok but I'd still be keen to come in and speak with you. I'm sure my wife would too."

"Definitely. If I can call you in a few days we should have a clearer picture by then. Anyway, sorry to have troubled you at work, I won't keep you any longer."

"No, no, it's no trouble at all. Thank you for phoning."

"You're welcome."

"Bye then." And he hung up the phone.

"Bye Dad," I said and I hung up too. Looking back, of all the things that went wrong that week, it's that phone call that I regret the most.

"Blimey, you've been in the wars. What happened to you?" asked the lady as I approached the counter in Village Cafe.

"Skiing accident," I replied glibly and ordered an all-day breakfast and a cup of coffee. They served two types; black and white. Staring out of the window, my thoughts drifted towards the meeting the next day. The shares would be bought by me, in my name and remain untouched for the next 20 years. By then I would own a piece of some of the largest companies on the planet. Just thinking about it my excitement grew. I was sitting on a fortune; it seemed so close I could almost spend it. I felt like I had the winning lottery ticket but I couldn't cash it in until the office opened on Monday morning. Whatever the effects, by November 2005, I'll be made. Fuck living in a damp flat, fuck the suspension, fuck being on my own and finally fuck drifting. I could take control. So much for astrology, it turns out you don't need to know the future, just how to go back and change the past. My lunch arrived, disturbing my revelry. "One bacon, sausage and tomato. Sauces are over by the cutlery," said the waitress who smiled from behind a red and white apron.

"Thanks." I wasn't going to mess this up. It was a gift and I was going to make the most of it. Outside, a brown Allegro pulled up by the curb. A middle-aged man got out and put some money in the meter before hurrying off to the shops. He was about the age my Dad was when he died. I looked back down towards my plate. The saddest thing about the accident was how it had left Mom. The last time we talked about him was on his birthday last year, we had looked at some old photos and she'd told me about the night they'd first met. I knew the story word for word, but it was still lovely to see her face light up as she told us how handsome he looked in his white jacket. But then I think she remembered why we were talking about him. She started to cry a little and I touched her shoulder. Linda came down from upstairs and rushed forward to give her a hug. I felt embarrassed because I didn't know what to do, I was never good at that stuff, so I went into the kitchen and put the kettle on. I stayed in there until the sobbing stopped. The bloke sitting in front of me got up and a sharp breeze blew through as he left. It was beginning to get dark. I finished my dinner and asked for another cup of coffee. I wished that I could just phone the client in Dudley and cancel my Dad's appointment the next day, but I had no way of knowing who he was going to meet. I thought again about trashing his car but then thought about spending time in prison until the early '90s. I didn't know what to do. I needed to change the single biggest event of my entire life with the minimum impact on everything else. And I needed to do it before tomorrow.

As I stared out of the window, the streetlights began to come on. He'll be getting home from work in a few hours, I thought. He'll come in, hang his coat up by the door and throw his keys on the side by the phone. He'll carry his tea into the front room and watch Midlands Today before helping Dave and I with our homework. Later, if there is nothing on telly he'll fall asleep in the armchair or do the crossword before nodding off. He'll be up and away early tomorrow morning and only Mom will see him off. He'll be tired after the party and sitting up with me at the hospital and he'll already look forward to Saturday's lie-in. He'll try to fend off his lethargy with an extra cup of coffee. The roads will be busy leading up to the M5 and the constant drizzle and heavy surface water will make it hard to see. He'll have the radio on listening for the news and weather. In the minutes before the crash the rain will become heavier and the windows will begin to steam-up. He'll get hot in his coat

159

and suit jacket and as the traffic slows he'll begin to worry about making it there on time. He'll flick his wipers up to full speed and the noise and steady rhythm will dull his concentration. Stuck in traffic he'll pay the price for his second coffee and fidgeting in his seat he'll debate whether to try and find a garage with a toilet. He'll look at his watch. He'll be over taken by a sports car that he liked. A pretty looking passenger in the next car will catch his eye. He'll change radio stations. He'll have chest pains. A car will swerve in front of him. His eyes will close for a second. We don't know what happened in the moments leading up to the crash. The police report said he left his lane, crossed the centre-line and drove into the path of an on-coming lorry. It all happened in a crucial second. And just as I finished my coffee it hit me. I didn't need to change the past, just one second of it. I didn't need to stop him crashing, just keep him at home. Put him in a different place in a different time. If I stole his car there could be no car crash. At this late stage, I thought, it was the perfect plan; perfect barring two problems. Firstly, I couldn't drive.

"That doesn't matter," I told myself. "I've had enough lessons."

Ok, but secondly, I didn't know the first thing about stealing cars. I didn't have time to learn how to break into a car without attracting attention. So, how do I do it?

"I get the keys?" But how? Come on Martin, I urged myself. "How do I get the keys?" Think. Think. "If I wait until everyone is asleep, it would be easy to just pick them up from where Dad leaves them by the phone. That's it.

Although, I'd need to get into the house first."

"Fuck," I said loudly, prompting the man next to me to look up from his egg and chips. Suddenly I knew it. I felt sick. "I can't." But I do, I've already done it. I slid the knife from my empty plate and into my jacket pocket.

"Oh boy," I thought. "I'm going to mug myself."

Chapter Fifteen

I went back to Andrew Warrender's house that day after school to copy some computer games. His sister Jenny was in Sixth Form and his Dad designed parts for aeroplanes. That's all I remember about Andrew Warrender. It was the first and last time I ever went to his house. The games were for the Commodore 64 and we copied them tape-to-tape on his sister's hi-fi. I never got to play those games; they were taken along with everything else in my bag. I always thought that if my Dad hadn't died, everyone would have made a bigger deal about the mugging, they acted as if I'd just been picked-on by some other kid rather then threatened with a knife by a deranged maniac. 20 years later though, as I walked to the scene from the other direction, I finally understood what had happened. I looked down at the dark grey jacket I've seen in my nightmares a thousand times since. I knew what I'd say and what would be said in return. But despite the horror that I was responsible, a part of me actually felt relieved. For all those years I'd wondered what would have happened if the mugger had used the blade he was wielding, when the truth was it had been a butter knife. I used to be terrified that if he hadn't been scared-off I would have been killed, but I now knew I had never been in danger. I thought about all the times that I'd decided not to do something, just in case it would happen again. The times I'd seen that familiar face everywhere I looked: hidden within crowds; walking behind me on a dark night; lurking in a doorway. How can I do this knowing what it'll do to my life, I wondered as I waited at the traffic lights to cross? How do you justify an act knowing with such clarity the affects it will have? But there was no debate, I do justify it, it has happened. I hurried along Deakin Drive. And anyway, I told myself, it's the only way I can stop something even worse. I headed through the precinct and out towards the park. I looked at my watch and thought for a second I was going to be late, but how could I be? It was bitterly cold now but I walked with a determined stride and sweat built-up on my back. My Mom said that it had probably been fifth years messing around and that she'd phone the school the next day if my bag didn't turn up. I remember getting home, out of breath, tears streaming down my cheeks, trying to picture his face, his clothes, his voice so that I could give a good description to the police. I wondered if there was going to be anything on the news about it the next day like that woman who'd been mugged in Mere Green. It had never made any sense to me why he'd wanted my bag. Apart from the two computer games, there was my music folder, my history homework, some pens, some pop, my keys and my glasses. I think the fact that I couldn't make sense of it was the reason it had such an impact on my life; if something so unexpected could happen like this, it means that anything could happen at any point. As I walked to the scene of the crime, I found it impossible to comprehend. Of all the possible scenarios I'd worked over from that day, being mugged by my older self, whilst on a secret time-travel mission from the future had never surfaced once. I'd always thought it must be drugs, but

164

I never knew why a drug addict would want the chords to The Largo and a diagram of 16th century crop rotation. I felt a sense of calmness as I reached Park View. If getting mugged never really happened then maybe things weren't so bad after all. As I reached the turning I had to concentrate. I had to become the man who would inspire fear for years to come. I turned the collar up on my coat and marched confidently into the alley.

"Christ knows if I can pull this off," I muttered, even though I knew that I did. That's why it made no sense to agonise over it, that's why I left the café and made my way straight there. As I took a deep breath, a feeling of dread filled my body, like I was about to make the worst mistake of my life. But in the dim light ahead I could see myself approaching, and I had no time to think this through.

"Sorry kid. You'll understand," I whispered as I lingered by one of the back fences pretending to look in my pockets for something. I was 30 yards away and I could see my Parka hood was up against the wind. 15 yards, I sniffed and screwed up my face to look menacing. Ten yards and I went over my lines. Five yards away and I shouted.

"Hey kid gimme your fucking bag or I'll kick your fucking head in."

They were the 13 words that would alter the way I looked at life forever. It felt like I was in a film.

"What?" I was shocked. I looked so small.

"Gimme your fucking bag." I said with a growl, stepping closer. How was I suddenly this person?

"But I need it." I stepped away.

"I've got a knife," I said, pulling the blade from my pocket. "And I'll cut your fucking face open." Even as the words came out of my mouth, I couldn't believe what I was saying. I looked really scared now but I was still holding the bag. "Give it here." I lurched forward and just like I remember, just like it was scripted, I grabbed the bag. I tried to hang on to it but I wasn't strong enough. I got pushed to the ground and fell against the railings. I cut my hand on the concrete and put it up to my mouth. I looked up as he towered above me, his cut lip and blackened eye. I saw the knife in his long fingers, the crazed desperation on his pale face, the stench of his breath as he leaned towards me. He looked as if he hesitated for a second, wanting to say something or do something to me. I'd seen it from both sides now and I realised I had wanted to say something, I'd wanted to say, 'Don't worry Martin, you'll understand one day' but I didn't, I couldn't seem to change anything about it. I picked up the bag and Rachel appeared on cue.

"Oi," she shouted and we both looked across. "Leave him alone." It was at that very moment, sitting on the alleyway floor that I fell in love with Rachel Dixon. I turned and ran, clutching the bag to my chest, the feeling of horror at what I'd just done making me gasp for breath. She ran over and reached out her hand to me. She was wearing a red ski jacket. "Are you alright?" she asked, but I didn't say anything. I stood up and was still holding her hand.

"You're Martin Brownlow. You got mugged."

I nodded.

"What happened, are you alright?" I tried to explain but no

words came out. She took my arm. "You're shaking."

"I know."

"Are you gonna be alright?"

"He took my bag," was all I managed to say.

 "I saw." And with a tenderness I can still feel to this day she brushed the hair across my forehead. For a second I could feel her breath, it smelt of mints and cigarettes. I thought she was going to kiss me.

"I've gotta go," was all she said and she left me there alone in the alleyway. I saw her hundreds of times at school after that but she never mentioned that moment. In fact we had never spoken again until she stood at the chicken counter at Thompson's that morning, 20 years later.

Chapter Sixteen
Friday November 11th 2005

I left my school bag at the bus stop in 1985. I don't know who had it but it never found its way back to me. I'd thought about leaving it for myself in my house later to try to ease some of the horror I'd just caused, then I realised that would only freak myself out more. I only went back to the flat for a few hours to rest, bathe my eye and pick up the rest of the money for the next day. All being well I'd catch a train to London first thing and return a millionaire. If everything worked out I wouldn't be coming back to this flat, possibly ever. My Dad is alive, I make all this money, why would I come back here? If I ever lived here at all. I probably won't remember anything about this place. I hated and loved that flat in equal measure. Looking around my front room, it was a testament to 21st century bachelordom. I had never gotten around to decorating properly, why would you when you were renting, I asked myself, it just adds value to someone else's property? So instead the film posters that had gone up early-on to hide the wood-chip had become permanent fixtures. Above the TV, George Clooney and Jennifer Lopez looked down from the poster of Out of Sight. The Alex Ross collectors' edition artwork from Unbreakable hung Blu-tacked to the door. I'd meant to get a frame for them years ago. Black and white stills from Mission Impossible, Goldeneye and The Hudsucker Proxy were behind the sofa and pride of place beside the bookshelf stood a colour screen-grab from Empire Strikes Back signed by actor

Jeremy Bulloch. The bookshelf itself was crammed. I'd spent more on DVDs in the past four years than on holidays and nights out. I loved my film collection, I could lose hours taking them down and examining the cases or reading the production notes. If I wasn't in the mood for watching something, I'd rearrange them in chronological order, by actors or by my favourite directors. Almost 1000 films, not including copies or downloads and there'd still be times when there was nothing I fancied watching and I'd have to traipse to the video shop. Would I still have my beloved collection in my new life? I wolfed down a plate of sausages and beans to give me energy for the night ahead and packed my bag. I wanted to travel light but there was a lot to bring. The money alone, almost £12,000, took up half of my backpack, while my shoes, shirt and trousers for the meeting virtually filled it. Looking down at the banknotes it felt as if I was preparing for a secret assignment, and as I folded my clothes I imagined the details of the night to come. In my head getting Dad's car keys became a daring mission to retrieve top-secret code-breaking equipment from a well-guarded foreign embassy. The train ride to London would be a risky escape through communist Russia using forged papers, and the appointment with the broker became an undercover pay-off to a former KGB general who had aspirations of becoming the next Soviet President. I was putting my life on the line for my country again, having used the train through Siberia scenario many times on the way to work on dark winter mornings. It was 21.00 hours. I'd have to leave at half nine, The General was not a man to keep

170

waiting. I glanced around the flat, my 'safe house' after a thousand successful missions to the paper shop. I felt a sudden sadness at the thought of leaving my flat for good. I walked over to the window to see if it had stopped raining. Across the street a black Mondeo caught my eye. It was parked at the darkest point between two streetlights. On the drivers' side a man sat reading the paper. I closed the curtains to all but a slight gap and peered out. Maybe I'm under surveillance? Most likely one of The General's men sent out to oversee the exchange. Or it could be a bloke waiting for his wife. I had to get going. I closed the door for the last time, lingering a second with my hand on the doorframe before taking a deep breath and stepping out into the street. As I crossed onto Malcolm Avenue the Mondeo drove past me and up to the High Street. I looked to my left and whispered into my collar: "Black Rook, this is White Night. Have a possible tail. Please advise."

And then I felt embarrassed. I'd done the whole MI6 thing a million times but as a distraction from commuting and an escape from serving chickens for 17 grand a year. It was a bit of excitement on an otherwise uneventful day. But today was far from average, it was pretty fucking exceptional. I was about to travel to the past for the second time that day, wasn't that enough? Maybe that's what comes of leading a boring life, I thought, no sense of occasion.

Chapter Seventeen

Sunday August 26th 1984

Marc McKirdy, one of my friends from junior school, came over to stay one night in the summer holidays, we were both 12. We were allowed to sleep in the tent in the back garden, like my brother had done with his friends a few years earlier. We had food, torches and a radio and I brought out some books and magazines. My Mom said we could play music until 9pm by which time she assumed we'd tell ghost stories and rude jokes and get off to sleep. When she came out to check on us at half ten we pretended to be asleep and I heard her whisper to us good night. Marc waited about 20 minutes after my parents' bedroom light went off before telling me we were going out. Straight away I didn't want to go. It was the first time I'd had someone over and I really liked it. I knew my Dad would go spare if he found out, but Marc wore me down. The final straw was when he told me he and Dean Sawyer had gone out 'exploring' when he stayed over at his and as far as I was concerned, I was no more of a bottler than Deano was. I thought my Mom would wake up as we unzipped the tent. The noise seemed to shatter the peaceful August night but no lights came on. We trod carefully across the back lawn and eased open the latch on the back gate. As soon as we were out into the street it was like another world. There we were, out alone at night. I remember how quiet the whole neighbourhood felt and we sniggered to ourselves at the thought of being awake while everyone else was fast asleep. I was so excited. I couldn't wait to get back to school and tell everyone what we'd done. We ran out of my road and into Tudor Hill Drive. I thought the sound of our footsteps slapping on the pavement would wake the whole street. It was a warm night and in the rush to get dressed I hadn't put any socks on under my trainers. For me, just being out was enough, it was the highlight of an already great night, but Marc's attention span was short and he had already moved on to something new and more mischievous. We ran past a dark-coloured Sierra and just as he drew level with the driver's window he grabbed the wing mirror and pulled it out at an angle. He laughed. I was terrified, what if it had had an alarm? Those kinds of cars sometimes did. He did the same thing at the next car, and the next and I was sure that if the noise didn't attract attention then Marc's victorious cackle would. He shouted at me to do one as he ran back in my direction, targeting the passenger side mirrors.

"You'll break one," I warned him.

"I won't," was all he replied. I really didn't know what to do. I didn't want to do it but I didn't want him telling people at school that I bottled it and spoil my moment. I had just about talked myself into joining him when he called out to me from down the street.

"Look at this."

He was standing outside one of the big houses; it had a large metal gate at the end of the driveway.

"What?" I asked, dreading the answer as my heart still pounded from his last stunt.

"A note," he said.

"What note?"

"There, in the milk bottle."

"Oh yeah." I could see it but I didn't understand.

"Go and get it."

"No. Why?"

"To see what it says."

"It'll be to the milkman."

"I know. Go and get it."

"They'll wake up." I said, looking up at the house.

"Go quietly then."

"Why don't you go and get it?"

"Because it's my idea."

"So?" And then it was like he had read my mind.

"Why are you being such a chicken?" he asked.

"I'm not."

"You are.

"I'm not."

"Then go and get it."

There was the slightest creak as I inched the gate open. It may as well have been an air raid siren.

"Shhh," whispered Marc. Not wanting to open the gate fully I slipped sideways through the narrow gap and tip-toed across the gravel driveway. My Dad had told me about those new lights that come on when people walk past and I willed them not to have one. Bending down at the front door there was no sense of excitement, just absolute fear. I held my breath, pulled the note from the bottle and sprinted back to the gate. We both bolted away leaving the gate unlatched and we were half way down the street before we stopped to examine our prize.

"Give it here," Marc said and I handed it over. He read it aloud.

"Gary, no milk for two weeks from the 27th of August to the 10th of September. Thanks, Number 43."

Was that it? I couldn't believe it. All that for a boring note. Marc chuckled.

"What?" I asked getting slightly annoyed.

"Come with me." We ran into Lyndon Drive, him in front, me struggling to keep up. Marc held out the note and surveyed the houses. I looked on trying, to second-guess him. Number 37, number 39, number 41.

"Here." He stood outside number 43, beckoning me over.

"No way," I told him. There was not a chance.

"Go on."

"No. You do it this time."

"It's your note, you got it."

"Exactly, that's why you should do this," I told him.

"Go on. It'll be really funny. They won't have any milk for two weeks. And the other people will have it going bad on their doorstep."

"I'm not doing it, the Milkman might get sacked."

"He won't. Go on. If you do this then I'll do something worse."

"What?"

"You'll see. Go on Brownie."

"I'm not-"

"I'll tell everyone at school," he goaded.

"I don't care," I told him but he knew I did.

"You could have done it by now."

"I'm not doing it."

"Why are you such a bottler?"

There was no gate this time, just an open driveway with a Volkswagen parked on it. I was there and back in seconds. I rolled up the paper and crept forward. The note slotted-in perfectly and I dashed away. Marc was already running ahead of me. He turned the corner and was standing by the bus stop by the time I joined him. We both laughed. Him out of excitement, me out of nerves. I knew it was wrong but what was I supposed to do? I wanted to go home now.

"Let's go back," I suggested looking at my watch. "It's nearly midnight."

"Not yet."

"Why?"

"I've still gotta do my dare."

"Oh. Don't worry about it. You did the cars."

"It won't take a second. Wait here and get ready to run," he warned as he disappeared back around the corner leaving me sitting at the bus shelter wondering what he was up to. I was reading the graffiti when I heard him come back.

"Look out," he yelled and I turned just as he launched a brick at the glass. It hit a second later, shattering the bus shelter window into thousands of pieces and causing a deafening crash. Bits of glass fell around me, as I stood rooted to the ground. What had he done? Why had he done it? Where was he? I ran off in the direction I could see Marc fleeing. We only made it half way up Oak Hayes Road before the blue light appeared. I knew immediately what it was, and stopped running. I think I even thought that the police would shoot me if I didn't. They didn't take us to the station, just to our parents. We had to pay the council half each to replace the window but thankfully it didn't go any further. I wasn't allowed out for the rest of the holidays and it took a week before my Mom and Dad spoke to me properly. It was my first and only run-in with the police and if nothing else it kept me on the straight and narrow. So I was surprised at how cool I felt now about breaking into my house that night. That was probably the problem; I thought of it as my house. But in actual fact, I'd threatened a 13-year-old boy with a knife, taken his keys and was entering his home in the middle of the night to steal his Dad's car as his family slept in their beds.

Chapter Eighteen

Tuesday November 12th 1985 – 1.18am

The night was quiet, a lot like that time with Marc only much colder. I'd dressed fully in black, and if nothing else I looked the part. Standing outside my house again I sensed none of the sentimentality I'd felt a few days before. I was almost business-like as I walked around to the back of the house, surveying the windows for lights and sounds. My pulse began to quicken as I took the keys from my trouser pocket and as I opened the gate and trod carefully across the grass it felt like tumbling into a rabbit hole. Looking back now I have to concentrate to stop the events that would follow from blurring into a whirlpool of thoughts and feelings. If I'd stopped at that point then everything could have been different, but in truth I couldn't have stopped, even if I'd have wanted to. The key barely made a sound as I inserted it into the backdoor, but I still waited almost a full minute before I began the slow anti-clockwise turn. I knew to lift the door as I opened it into the kitchen to ensure it was silent. Even in the pale moonlight I could make-out the red and white tiles and colour-coordinated kettle and toaster. The blinds were down and that night's dishes stood washed and dried on the draining board. Walking through the kitchen it felt like I was visiting a relative's house after spending years away. It was smaller than I remembered. The table, used mostly just for Sunday roasts and Christmas dinners, almost filled the side by the back window. Looking at it through the dark I pictured where we sat, the same places every time. Dad at the end, by the dresser, Mom and I on one side, Dave and Linda on the other. I vaguely remember a time when I sat next to Dave but we fought a lot so I was moved. We had all our celebrations around that table. Pulled crackers and blew out candles. Some Sunday mornings my Mom would do breakfast and I'd wake up to the smell of bacon and eggs. I'd run down just as a full-English was being served. Mom and Linda argued sometimes; so, when he couldn't get them to stop, Dad would tell her she was allowed to take her dinner up to her room. The rest of us would eat in silence until Mom calmed down again. But most of the time Sundays would be family time, and it was often the only occasion the five of us would all eat together, taking our positions around that table. I don't even know what happened to it when Mom sold the house. It was too big for her new place. If I don't manage to change things, I thought, then we've already had our last meal around that table. I've already seen him for the last time and he and Mom are mid-way through their last night together. I took a deep breath. No car, no car crash. I was there; I was changing time, minute-by-minute. There were two of me, one fast asleep in bed, the other skulking around downstairs changing time. The clock above the fridge read 1.35am and I wondered where my Dad would be tomorrow morning. At the police station probably and phoning his client to rearrange the meeting for some time the next week. I wondered if we'd go away on holiday together next year and where we would go. But then I got that nagging feeling again. If it happened why

180

didn't I remember it yet? Give it time, I thought. Concentrate on what you're doing.

I knew the kitchen door was going to pose the biggest danger. Open it too slowly and it creaked, too quickly and one of the hinges had a tendency of coming away from the doorframe. I'd done it successfully lots of times, sneaking down for biscuits or a drink when I should have been in bed, but I was 20 years out of practice. I pressed the handle down as far as it would go and closing my eyes I teased the door open. I felt the slightest pull of resistance, the creak. Sliding my fingers into the open gap I placed my right palm flat on my side. I actually counted to three before flipping the door towards me, fast enough to beat the creak, but then slowing it to a smooth stop before the hinge went. It was silent and the biggest hurdle was safely jumped. I knew if left ajar it would swing back and creak at the same spot so, after looking for a suitable prop, I reached a cookbook down and eased it into place. The light from the street flooded in through the porch and illuminated the hallway. When I couldn't see the keys on the phone table I moved some papers hoping they would be underneath. I then looked on the floor to see if they had been knocked off, but still no sign. I told myself to stay calm and carefully reached inside my Dad's jacket hanging on the coat hook. I searched the pockets four times but nothing. Fuck. Stay calm. I checked them again. This was bad. He would come home, jacket by the door, keys by the phone. It was like clockwork. Calm down. Think this through. He never left them in the front room. They're not in his jacket. Then where? His trousers?

The ones most probably lying on his bedroom floor. This was too much. How the hell was I supposed to do this? I took the first step up the stairs, placing weight on the side nearest the wall. Second step. Someone's going to wake up. Third and fourth. At least Dad slept nearest to the door. Fifth step. Mom's a really light sleeper though. This is crazy. Miss the sixth. Do I grab the keys and sneak out or do I grab them and run? Seventh and eighth. I wish I could just explain, 'excuse me; you die in a car crash in a few hours' time'. I stood on the ninth step and then the tenth. I was hardly breathing. Eleventh. It creaked. I froze to the spot. I stood there for three minutes. Twelfth. The last one and I was on the landing. The bathroom light was on, a throwback to when we were kids. I walked past my room. Mom and Dad's was the next door. At six feet away I was already reaching for the handle. My hand began to shake but I'd come too far not to see it through. The door was open an inch and I slowly pushed it wider. I stood in the doorway for a second before I stepped in. There wasn't a sound. I touched the Anaglypta wallpaper. It smelt like my parents' room, it took me back in time. I could be bringing them breakfast in bed for Mother's Day or waking them up to get an early start on our Christmas presents. My Dad was snoring; my Mom was facing the opposite wall. In the dim light I could see my Dad asleep, he wasn't wearing his glasses. He didn't wear them in the funeral parlour either and everyone said he didn't look right. I crouched to my knees and padded softly around the floor, my eyes trained on my Mom and Dad three feet away. I touched his belt first and

182

gently dragged his trousers closer. Pressing against the material I could feel some change and his wallet. I moved to the other pocket. Neither of them stirred. The other side felt heavier. I slid my hand inside and my fingers sensed his keys. I had them. Keeping them tightly bunched together I pushed them into my back pocket before standing up and inching away. I stood in the doorway for a second and watched them sleeping. I knew if it didn't work it would be the last time I saw him, and the last time my Mom would be the way she used to be. I wished them both good night and crept away. With the cookbook back in place there was no trace that I'd ever been there and as the cold air turned my breath to steam I marched quietly across the garden. As I passed the front of the house it was as still as I had left it ten minutes before. They'll never know I was there and they'll never know how things could have been. I hoped Dad's car would start without any trouble; it could be temperamental in the cold. I might have to let it run for a minute but it didn't matter. The chances of them hearing it were pretty slim and even if they did come down I could drive away. I still didn't know where I was going to dump the car but I could figure that out later. I was so composed as I walked to the car that I almost ignored the police officers at first, it took a moment to register who it was. I still don't know if someone called them or if they were on patrol but for the second time in my life I was escorted to a police car.

Chapter Nineteen

Tuesday November 12th 1985 – 3.46am

"I'll ask you one more time. Where did you get the money?" growled DCI Bruce, in no mood for any more games. I decided to come clean.

"I won it." It was the first thing I'd said since I'd been brought in. "Just from betting shops. The horses and that."

"Ok, good. Now seeing as you're talking, would you mind telling us what your name is?" What the hell could I tell him?

"Am I going to get bail?" I asked.

"How can we bail you if we don't know who we're bailing," cut in DC Matthews.

He had a good point.

"I can't say anymore. I haven't done anything wrong," I told them.

"Ok," said Matthews. "Then what happened to your face? Looks like you got quite a beating off someone."

I nodded and thought about the other night.

"Who was it? Someone you know?"

"It's complicated. You wouldn't...."

"Try us. Start with your name so we at least know who we're talking to."

I knew I had to give them something.

"Sylvester." I said.

"Sylvester? Is that your first or second name," pressed Bruce.

"First."

"And your second name?" What the hell.

"McCoy."

"For the tape the suspect has identified himself as Sylvester McCoy. Well Mr McCoy, my name is Detective Constable Iain Mathews; this is Detective Chief Inspector Neil Bruce."

"And you are about to tell us why you're walking the streets in the middle of the night with twelve thousand pounds in cash about your person," ordered Bruce.

I was driven in by a Sergeant and a WPC, who picked me up outside of my house. If I'd have handled it better I might have walked free but I fell to pieces at the first line of questioning.

"Evening. Where you headed?" the Sergeant asked.

"Just home," I told him.

"And where's that?"

"Just around the corner."

"It's late, where have you been?" added the WPC.

"Oh, just, you know. Couldn't sleep. Fancied a walk."

"What's in the bag?" she followed up.

"Just my work things." I smiled and went to carry on walking.

"Would you mind hanging on a minute Sir?" the Sergeant said, before speaking something into his radio. Of everything that happened after that, the only good thing was that I threw my Dad's keys. Just as the Sergeant turned to acknowledge his response and a second before the WPC got out of the passenger side door I tossed them into the bushes at the edge of our lawn. So they arrest me, I thought, so they take the money, I could still come back and steal the car. And if not, my Dad would have to find his keys before setting off, which would slow him down if not prevent him from going altogether. I just hoped it would be enough. The WPC found the cash on first inspection. I tried to explain about my meeting but they didn't buy it. I went along for questioning to avoid arrest but refused to answer them in the car. What the hell could I tell them? I told myself it was just questioning; I think I was over simplifying it. I was signed-in and handed over to CID. The interview room was small and bare and almost full by the time the three of us were in it. Things started politely enough but the mood changed when I refused to give them my details. I told them I'd done nothing wrong but they kept up the questioning. Who owned the money? Where was it from? What was I doing with it? What had happened to my face? Bruce was the older of the two and ex-Army judging by his build and manner. No nonsense and hard looking. He loved the fact that I was clearly out of my depth. Mathews was my age and my build, although slightly fitter looking. He was pale faced and bookish and had glasses and a soft Welsh accent. I initially waived my right to a solicitor thinking the less people that got involved the easier it would be to sort things out. I changed my mind after I was arrested.

"Did you rob somebody?" asked Bruce.

"No."

"Then where did it come from?"

"I told you I won it."

"Well I don't believe you Mr McCoy. Who were you meeting

in London?" They found a timetable in my bag.

"I was buying shares."

"You don't have an address but you were buying shares?"

"Yes. No. I just don't have one at the moment."

"You told the officers you couldn't sleep. Where were you staying? Who were you staying with?" And it went on. Relentless questioning followed by wafer-thin replies.

I wanted to tell them nothing as every response got me deeper into trouble.

"Do you want to go to prison Mr McCoy?" threatened Bruce.

"For what? I haven't done anything"

"We have reason to believe you obtained the money through illegal means."

"Well I didn't. What proof do you have that I've done anything wrong?"

The questioning continued. There was a knock at the door. A WPC entered the room.

"I've got the information from Lloyd House, you asked for Guv," she told Bruce.

"Thanks." He got up and left the room.

"For the tape DCI Bruce has left the room," said Matthews into the tape recorder. It was the same kind I used to use in front of the telly to record Top of the Pops.

A few moments passed, neither of us spoke.

"For the tape, DCI Bruce has re-entered the room." he said again.

"Six foot tall, medium build, short black hair. Eyes, green. Early to mid-30s. Local accent. Clean shaven. Seen wearing a black t-shirt with the words Ben Folds Five on the front and a grey coloured jacket. Does this gentleman sound familiar to you?" asked Bruce, reading from a dot-matrix computer print-out. I said nothing.

"For the tape the suspect has refused to answer," said Matthews.

Bruce continued. "Seen on two occasions carrying a black Reebok rucksack. A bit like this one." He lifted up my bag.

"For the tape DCI Bruce is showing Mr McCoy a black bag." He carried on reading.

"Suspect has visited at least 12 betting offices since Saturday 9th November. Cashiers from three separate betting shops contacted police because of the large sums of money and the gentleman's 'suspicious behaviour'." He left a long silence. "So you were telling the truth," he added.

"Yes. Yes. I was. Thank you. Does this mean I can go now please?" I said excitedly.

"No Mr McCoy it means we have reason to suspect you are involved in a conspiracy to obtain money by deception."

"What?"

"Fraud, Mr McCoy."

For the tape I was completely shocked.

"Do you know Donald Frasier?" asked Bruce.

"No."

"He's a racehorse owner. Well connected, he was arrested two weeks ago for horse doping."

"I don't know him."

"Then tell us Mr McCoy how you won eight grand this week backing 24 of his horses?"

189

"I just bet on them that's all. I don't know him."

"Then why were you picked up by officers with a bag full of money half-a-mile away from his house?"

I had nothing to say. The familiar sense of dread crept over me.

"Sylvester." Matthews said. "It's late, we're all tired but we are going to start needing some answers from you soon because come the morning it won't be us asking the questions."

"Who then?"

"We'll hand you over to West Midlands Fraud Squad," he explained.

"The morning? But I need to get out tonight, I need to get bail or something."

"That's not going to happen. You'll be interviewed by the Fraud Squad at 8am."

"Seriously, this is important. I need to get out tonight."

"Nobody's going anywhere tonight. You need to start cooperating."

For the tape I'd stopped listening. I actually thought I was going to cry. Bruce would have loved that. My Dad dies on Tuesday November 12th. I can still remember it happening. It's five hours away. If I've stopped it then why could I still remember it? Maybe I've changed nothing so far, but at least there's still time, except I was sitting here talking about horse racing. He's not going to die, I promised myself. Not after all this. I'll figure it out.

Bruce was still talking: "...... time is now 3.46am. For the tape, the suspect has refused to answer further questions.

We're going to suspend the interview pending further investigation."

Matthews leant forward and pressed stop on the tape recorder. Both men stood up. I needed to think of something quickly. And it would have to be something drastic. I had a flash of inspiration. It would get me in deeper but it was the only card I had left to play. Desperate times, desperate measures. They were just about to leave when I called them back.

"Detectives," I shouted. They both looked back. I took a deep breath.

"I'd like to confess to a murder."

Chapter Twenty
Tuesday November 12th 1985 – 5.11am

Malcolm Barrowclough, the duty solicitor was a red-faced 60-something who sat and listened patiently as I laid down the terms.

"We go tonight or not at all," I explained. "I'll take DC Mathews and only DC Matthews to the spot. I want the others at least 100 yards away."

"They'll never agree to that," Barrowclough protested.

"Well it's your job to make them agree. And I go without handcuffs."

"No, that'll never happen. You've admitted to a murder, they aren't going to let you just run around unrestrained."

"Fair enough." I had to agree. I'd be the first to complain if the police did allow that sort of thing to happen.

"I'll give full details as to how and why it happened after the body's recovered." Barrowclough nodded in agreement.

"One other thing, and this is important. At 8 'o clock this morning I need you to contact a man named George Brownlow."

Back in the interview room Barrowclough gave it to them like Costner in JFK.

"My client has clearly stipulated his conditions, if he's going to cooperate. You, I and the CPS know a signed confession is worth a bit of flexibility on your part Detective Chief Inspector Bruce."

"Flexibility. It'll take the Top Brass to say-so before we

193

organise a daytrip for a suspected murderer. And if he goes anywhere it'll be with a constable shackled to either arm. But before any of that happens we need a name."

"My client has clearly explained that he will only identify the body once it has been located."

"No. Not good enough. We need more information before anything happens. Who is it? Where is the body? Is it buried? Dumped? What did you do with it? How far is it from here?" Barrowclough turned to me.

"Five miles," I answered. "Maybe a bit less."

"Male or female?" asked Bruce.

"Detective, my client has clearly-"

"Female," I interrupted. It was 50/50 I suppose.

"And how was she killed?" Again all eyes fell on me but what was I meant to say? I'd never killed anyone so how did I know how I would've done it?

"I shot her," I said. What was I saying? Bruce looked unconvinced.

"How many times?" he asked.

"Three."

"Where?"

"In the head." Three shots in the head? I was sounding like a bloody maniac. "And in the body," I blurted out. "One in the head, two in the body." Jesus, now I sounded like a contract killer.

"And what was your relationship with the woman?" Bruce asked.

"Err. Platonic."

"So you knew her then?"

"Yeah. Vaguely. She was err.... Look I've said all I'm going to say at this point." I looked at Barrowclough for support.

"We need a name," Bruce continued.

"We're not going anywhere without one," interjected Matthews, it was the first thing he'd said in a while.

"My client-"

"Your client wants our cooperation as much as we want his," interrupted Bruce.

"My client-" he tried again. He was looking redder and a little out of breath.

Again Bruce cut-in: "Your client is looking at 15 years inside for the fraud charges alone." They were both really going at it now.

"We've made our intentions perfectly clear Detective Chief Inspector."

"And so have we. All we want is a name."

"And you will have one, after the body has been recovered," Barrowclough bellowed, looking like he was about to have a seizure.

"Until we get a name we don't even know if there is a body."

"And you are willing to risk that are you?"

"No, but I'm not willing to risk my officers-"

"Detective I have told you-"

"And I've told you we are not going anywhere without a name, so-"

"Jennifer Anniston," I blurted out and both men fell silent. I was genuinely worried Barrowclough was going to have a heart attack.

Mathews responded first: "Jennifer who?"

195

"Aniston," I clarified.

"The woman you claim to have murdered is called Jennifer Aniston?" asked Bruce.

"Yes," I replied calmly, as if he'd asked me if I like scrambled eggs. To this day I don't know where her name came from. I used to like Friends and she was in the papers a lot but of all the names I could have chosen I don't know why I chose hers.

"Check it," Bruce told Mathews. "For the tape DC Mathews has left the room," he added before turning to me with a look of absolute menace. "For your sake I don't know whether to hope there's a body out there or not."

"Are you threatening my client, Detective?"

"Of course not Mr Barrowclough, just offering him some free legal advice."

Tuesday November 12th 1985 – 6.51am

In the end it took a wake-up call to the Chief Superintendent to get the go ahead. Barrowclough was good. He remained strict with the police but he looked exhausted and was obviously as keen as everyone to get the whole thing resolved. I knew Bruce had his doubts. Missing persons only turned up one Aniston and that was a bloke called Carlos, last seen in Blackpool in 1976. And my story was far from convincing. Bruce would have known I was hardly a cold-blooded killer but at the same time he couldn't risk that I wasn't. If the truth be known after nearly 15 years on the Oven Counter I still didn't like cutting up raw chicken, but

196

he wasn't to know that, I could be one of those quiet geeky types who have a dark side. What if North Birmingham CID could turn a Neighbourhood Watch enquiry into a murder confession and retrieve the body in five hours, start to finish. It was the stuff that made careers and was far too good to pass-up. For Bruce it was worth disturbing the Chief Super in his mock-Tudor mansion in the early hours and it was why instead of sitting in a cell while my Dad was about to play chicken with an articulated lorry, I was riding in the back of a spacious police Rover on the way to 'the opening'. It was probably the heady concoction of adrenaline and unreality, but I was buoyant, almost feverish, as the convoy of police cars drove through the night. Feeling calmer I looked out of the window and tried to figure out how I was going to make it back to the 21st century without 40 coppers on my tail.

"Left here after the white van," I called out, directing the driver from the back seat. The PC at the wheel indicated and the six other marked cars in tow followed suit. Anyone who'd been up that morning would have wondered where the cavalcade of black and whites were going, but in truth so were the officers behind the wheel as I'd kept the location a guarded secret

"Straight on at the lights," I called from the backseat. I was handcuffed to DC Mathews, it was the best deal Barrowclough could broker. The flustered duty solicitor was supposed to accompany us on our early-hours excursion but he said he was having 'a funny turn' so stayed at the station. He said it was too much caffeine, but I felt genuinely concerned about his health. I tried to persuade him to go to the hospital, but a glare from Bruce refocused my attention to my very real situation. Matthews sat quietly beside me, resisting my attempts to chat. He even looked a little scared, and I suppose he probably was. All the police training in the world wouldn't prepare you for being singled out to accompany a killer back to the murder scene, even if the killer was really a supermarket supervisor, and a suspended one at that. I looked down at the handcuff on my right wrist and thought about how I had got there. I thought about 'the opening', about my Dad, about Shaun Byford and Sonia the Away-Days trainer. I thought about betting shops, about Elaine Baker, about the party and the mugging. I thought about Linda and Dave, and how desperately I'd tried to change things. I looked back out of the window as the streetlights flashed by. My mind raced. I closed my eyes for a second.

"Do you believe in fate Mathews?" I asked.

"What?" he sounded alarmed.

"You know, fate, destiny, that things happen for a reason?"

"This is not the time-"

"I don't know what I believe anymore. I mean, did this always happen? Did I always end-up here? It's weird, isn't it, to think that I'm here, not at home in bed. I wonder what you'd be doing now if I hadn't have come back." He didn't reply, I continued. "Sometimes you can see the influence you have over things, like ripples in a lake. I remember standing there the first time, thinking about going back, I'd never have guessed I'd have ended up here. Do you think-"

"Mr McCoy, please."

"Mr McCoy," I snorted. "I love that what I've told you is easier to believe than the truth."

"Are you saying you haven't told us the truth?"

"I don't think you could handle the truth. Has that been out yet? I don't think it has. 'You can't handle the truth!' You should look out for that one."

"Are you getting this Guv?" Matthews asked into his radio. There was a crackle of static before Bruce told him to ask me what I meant.

"It's just a film, that's all. It's not out yet." I fell silent. The convoy overtook a paperboy riding on his bike.

"Shit," I said out loud.

"What?" Matthews asked.

"The films. I forgot to record over the trailers," I said with a laugh. "People are gonna have a long time to wait for some of those."

"He's not making any sense Sir."

"That's right!" I said excitedly. "It doesn't make sense, none of it does. Even if you know everything, you still don't know *everything*..." I trailed-off. "I mean, it's not the information that's important, it's what you do with it. I knew what would happen but I didn't know *everything* that would happen? I mean, would things have happened anyway? That's the question I'm getting at. Take this murder for example, did it happen? Didn't it happen, the details are almost irrelevant, what's important is-"

"Guv, I think we should abort," Matthews called into the radio. Bruce told him to settle me down.

"I'm alright Brucie, just making conversation," I called out.

"Good game, good game," I laughed.

"I think-"

"Relax, I'm just passing the time. Passing through time, more like," I smiled, impressed by my wordplay. I felt tired and alert and terrified and euphoric. "Left at the lights up ahead," I called. "This is like Grand Theft Auto. This is wicked isn't it? I should have joined the police. Racing through the streets, kicking down doors. Do you get to do that? Straight on up ahead."

"Guv?" Matthews asked, his voice wavering. Bruce confirmed he was listening.

"Aw come on, chill-out. Do they say that now? Chill-out? I can't remember. That was one of the hardest bits, knowing what to say. Things change quickly, don't they? To be honest, I was never sure if I should even speak to people at all, you never know the affect it might have on their lives. What if I stopped someone to ask them the time, and that slowed them down, and then they missed their bus, and they were late for work and they got sacked, all because of me? That wouldn't be their fault; would it, because I shouldn't have been there? I know that probably wouldn't happen but just by being there and doing that meant that it could, do you know what I mean? I got chatting to a bloke in the bookies the other day, he was nice, he was a West Brom fan. But the whole time I kept wondering whether I was changing things. I was going to tell him who won the FA Cup next year but I decided not to. I wish I had now. His son was diabetic. I do know, you know. I could tell you whatever you want.

Liverpool, they beat Everton 3-1, Ian Rush gets two, I can't remember who scores the other one. Left up ahead, please. This is like directing the taxi driver from the backseat after you've been out." I paused for a second. "Taxi Driver, there's a film we *can* talk about, it's been out for ages. But we can't talk about Casino, that's not out yet. I've seen that hundreds of times. Well, not hundreds but a lot. I booked the day off work to see it. Right just here, please. Are you into films?"

"They don't have cinemas where you're going," Matthews said, trying to reassert himself over the situation.

"And where's that?"

"Prison Mr McCoy."

"Oh, I'm not going to prison. And even if I did, I'd escape. Poster on the wall, tunnel my way out with a rock hammer. 'I guess I just miss my friend'. I love that bit. Honestly, it's heartbreaking, and when they're down on the beach at the end. I always thought he should have killed his wife though, you know, for the redemption bit. Otherwise what does he have to redeem himself for? Being a bad husband? She cheated on him. Are you married?"

Matthews said nothing, just shot me a glare.

"No, that's not how it happens. You're supposed to be the good cop, the one who tries to build a rapport. Bruce is the dick. Sorry Bruce," I called out. "Straight on at the island. Do you say island? Some people say roundabout, I'm never sure which one it is, it's like alley or gully, are they the same? It's strange how there's more than one word for the same thing. Anyway, you're the good cop, he's the bad cop, that

201

bloke driving, PC 472, he's just an extra."

"And who are you?"

"That's more like it!" I said. "I'm the enigmatic stranger on a daring mission. Striving to put things right, surviving on my wits to stay two-steps ahead."

"Is that what you're doing?" Matthews sounded riled.

"Well yes. I know you don't think it but I'm not the villain of the piece."

"No?"

"No, I'm the sort of tragic anti-hero, I suppose. I don't fit the mold of the villain at all. He says it in Unbreakable. There are two kinds. The first is the soldier villain, the physical, henchman-type. You know, Jaws or Oddjob. They are hard to beat in a fight but they're not that clever. Then there's the real threat, the scheming, evil genius-type. They are smart and get others to do the dirty work. They manoeuvre themselves into place, sometimes taking years to fulfil what they want."

"And what's that?"

"The usual: money, power, their own little empire to control. But they are beatable, you just have to find their weakness. Turn right by the blue van, please. So I'm neither one of those. I can hardly run for the bus these days without feeling like I'm going to keel over and I nearly failed my A Levels. I'm not the villain sort. Anyway, I haven't done anything that bad. "

"You've confessed to a murder."

"Oh yeah. Good point. Right up ahead, please. We're almost there."

202

"Are you going to tell me where we are going yet?"

"To where it all ends, hopefully."

"And how does it end?"

"That's the beauty of it, I don't know. It might go bleak and disturbing or up-beat and optimistic."

"Which one are you hoping for?"

"Erm. I know it would be cooler to say the first one but if I'm honest I'm more Spielberg than Fincher. That said, I've given up trying to guess."

The rain began to fall and the driver activated the wipers. I thought about my Dad driving in the rain in a few hours time, drifting across to the opposite lane and being spread across the road by an articulated lorry. My last hope was Barrowclough making that call, there was nothing more I could do now.

"This has all been for something, you know."

"Yeah?"

"Yes. I want you to know, when you try to make sense of it all, that it was all for a good reason."

"That's what they all say."

"You're still not getting this are you? He's the cynic, the veteran cop who's seen it all, you're supposed to be the sympathetic rookie who can still see the humanity in the situation."

"Is this a game to you?"

"Not a game, a sort of thriller, I suppose, with Sci-Fi bits. You know, like at the end of... What would you have seen? I don't know, I can only think of modern ones. Was it a twist when you found out that Darth Vader is Luke's Dad? I can't remember, I think someone at school told me before I even saw it. Left up ahead, and then first right. You know what I'm on about? Luke's clinging on, Vader's just cut his right hand off. It's weird when you've got an iconic scene like that, you can't imagine life without it. Think of the day George Lucas wrote that on his typewriter, fucking hell that must have been amazing. Imagine him running and telling his wife. Then in three when Luke smashes Vader to the floor, always makes me feel sad, that bit."

"How much further?" Bruce called through the radio from the car behind.

"Not long Brucie Baby," I shouted back. "Anyway, what I'm trying to say is, you might not understand this, fuck, I don't understand it, but there is a point to it all. It'll be one of those you think about afterwards, you might not ever get it but at least there was an attempt to do something good, does that make sense?"

"If that's how you justify all this."

"Right at the island," I said, "Then pull-in by the church." And we were there. The risk had paid off. I'd dug myself in deeper in order to escape. I was actually quite proud of myself. I've gone to pieces hundreds of times in far less stressful situations. Matthews told Bruce that we were going through into the cemetery and we waited in the car while officers scattered to cover the exits.

"Now it's just us. I go with Mathews and I don't want to see another copper within 50 yards." I told Bruce, wondering why I was never this assertive when it came to claiming back time-in-lieu. He shot me a look of absolute disgust.

"I could still call this off," he warned.

"So could I," I replied.

"Don't try a fucking thing," he warned. "Or I will take personal responsibility to ensure you fall down a very large flight of stairs." I nodded, knowing he meant every word. We left the car park and entered the cemetery through the main gate, the rain still falling heavily. I knew the route well after my daily visits, more in five days than in 20 years. I was walking just ahead of Matthews, his left arm chained to my right. We passed the back of the church and headed down towards the burial plots. The air was cold and as we reached the big trees on the way to my Dad's prospective grave the heavens opened. The rain lashed against the headstones and streamed down our faces. We paused under a broken streetlamp, barely illuminated by the torches trained on us from the parameter.

"Why are we stopping? Where's the body?" Matthews called out, the rain causing his glasses to steam-up.

"This way," I shouted back, turning my head to shield my eyes from the downpour. Bruce's voice came through his radio and Mathew's replied that he was ok. We passed the bin and the water tap and left the path by the big broken cross. There was a clap of thunder. I felt my trousers begin to soak as we headed through the long grass.

"Where is it?" he called again.

"Over there."

As we walked towards the statue and its invisible opening to the future I played the final ace up my sleeve.

"Matthews," I called.

"What?"

"This murder. I didn't do it alone, I had help."

"What? From who? Guv, are you getting this?"

The radio crackled and Bruce confirmed that Matthews' mic was still recording the conversation.

"My mate, he helped me bury the body out here".

"Who is he?"

"His name is Shaun Byford, he's a mobile DJ."

"Suspect has named an accomplice. Last name Byford, first name Shaun?" The radio crackled again and Bruce repeated the name.

"You don't mess with people's sisters," I thought as I paused again, pretending to take a bearing from the fence in the distance. Honestly, at that point, handcuffed and surrounded by police, I had no idea what I would do when we reached 'the opening' but standing in the rain, facing a 30-year stretch and an unhealthy bout of police brutality I was as calm as a Hindu cow. I had no plan but I had the knowledge that it worked, whatever I was about to do. I knew and Linda knew, and after the other night her kids knew too, that there was a body in that cemetery and it was a matter of local folklore that the killer disappeared as if by magic. Everything had gone full-circle, not only do I get away but I become an urban legend, a way for kids to scare their younger brothers and sisters as they walk past St John's Church late at night. Matthews shouted to me again but for a second my attention was distracted. It was a glint of light that I spotted first, a dull reflection from one of the torches 50 yards away.

"Where is it?" he demanded to know, wiping his glasses with

206

his right hand. I stepped forward and pointed to the ground. "There." I told him and he turned towards his radio.

"Guv, we have a-"

I clenched my fist and hit him hard in the right eye. I was aiming for his nose. He screamed and all around me there was a burst of commotion. I crouched down quickly before leaping back up. In one motion I positioned myself behind Matthews, trowel in hand.

"I've got a knife," I screamed as police officers sprinted in our direction. "Stay back, all of you."

"Get him. It's a trowel," shouted Matthews.

"It's not. It's a knife and I'll slit his fucking throat." I warned, pushing Linda's trowel deeper into his neck.

"Urgh," he cried in pain.

"Put it down son, no one needs to get hurt." A voice called from a loud hailer in the darkness.

"I'll kill him if you don't stay back. I'll kill him"

"Ok. We're back. We're 50 yards back"

"Unlock me," I shouted at Matthews. "Tell him to unlock me," I yelled.

"Listen, put it down and we can-"

"I'll kill him, I swear to God I will."

"There's no way out, just-"

"He's a fucking dead man." I screamed at the figures in the distance, the heavy rain making them barely visible.

"Ok. Don't do anything stupid. Matthews do you have a key?" The voice asked, it's metallic sound reverberating off the headstones.

"Yes Sir," he shouted, slightly trembling.

"Unlock him," he was told and after a moment's fumbling he turned the key and released the cuff around my wrist.

"Now turn off all the torches," I shouted.

"There's nowhere to go." I was told.

"Do it," I screamed again. And the senior officer called the order through. The torchlight disappeared and the graveyard fell into darkness.

"Mathews," I said, "I'm really sorry about all this."

I drew the trowel up and hit him hard across the back of the head with the wooden handle. He dropped in a heap in front of me and I vaulted the fence and jumped through 'the opening'. Clutching the trowel I crouched behind the statue, waiting for a dozen coppers to come piling through time, but no-one emerged. It was still raining but I was back. I waited for what felt like hours before my heart rate returned to normal and I started to believe I may have actually done it. I'd escaped. I breathed out deeply and it was then that I remembered what my 'daring mission' had been in the first place. I turned to where my Dad's grave should have been. The small dark headstone was there. Still holding the trowel I walked around the front to read the inscription. I squinted in the dark and saw the familiar words. I'd done everything and changed nothing. He'd died 20 years ago today.

Chapter Twenty One

Saturday November 12th 2005

I still felt numb as I started pulling the weeds, and the steady
rhythm of the work seemed to lull me further into a trance.
As I dug over the soil by the headstone, I looked at my
Dad's name and his face flashed before me.
"I'm sorry Dad," I heard myself say. "I'm *so* sorry". My
breath caught in my throat. I'd failed him. I had the chance
to change everything but I hadn't made one difference. I
dropped the trowel to the ground as I put my head in my
hands and started to sob. Memories of my Dad flashed
before me: his face turning towards me with a grin, winking
at me across the room, building dens behind the sofa, his
face bursting with pride as I performed in a school play. As I
sat in the mud, oblivious to the cold and rain, I cried twenty
years worth of tears, my body shaking with the depth of
what I'd lost all over again.

I finished at the cemetery, caught the bus and was back at
my flat by 9.30am. Wet, cold and exhausted I walked
through the door, kicked off my shoes and picked up my
phone that had been left on charge by the telly. Playing back
my voicemails, Linda had called twice and Susan, Dennis'
PA, had rung to tell me to go in at 11.30am to see him after
his rounds.
I texted a reply to Linda: "Grave done looks good, I'll drop
off shears & trowel on way to hosp, cheers they helped lots,

love Mart."

I didn't reply to Susan. I was told it was an informal chat but I approached it as if it was a job interview. Dennis had news but Susan's efficiently ambiguous message hadn't given any hint as to whether it was good or bad. I steeled myself for both but wasn't sure what outcome I was hoping for most. All I knew was I was going in prepared.

"Vanilla Sky?" he said with scorn.

"Yeah," I confirmed.

"12 Monkeys?"

"My version's really old so it won't play properly."

"And Donnie Darko? Two out of three's not bad," said Andy, the video shop bloke in part approval, part disappointment. I was in a bit of a hurry but I went along with it.

"Where did I go wrong?"

"Like you have to ask. Freaking Jerking McGuire doing Sci-Fi. Vanilla Sky is terrible."

"I really like it," was as strong an argument as I had the energy to muster.

"Have you seen the Spanish original, Abre Los Ojos? Way better."

"I don't know. Sci-Fi McGuire ends with the line 'look at us. I'm frozen, you're dead, and I love you'. You can't beat dialogue like that."

The conversation went back and forth and I think the only thing that stopped me getting my membership revoked was a shared love of Terry Gilliam. I left him pricing down some ex-rental videos and headed out by the new releases. I was just about to exit when I noticed a sign by the door; it was next to a cut-out of The Bride wearing yellow Asics trainers. "You had any replies to this?" I called back.

"Two. But one said he was more into computer games and the other thought Brosnan was better than Moore."

"No luck then?"

"Naw. Not yet."

Even before 'the salmonella scandal', Susan hated me. She was very much a product of the new regime.

"He's not here, he's down in WD. You'll have to wait," she told me as I reported to her desk. She turned back to her computer and I sat in the waiting area. On the wall a large poster told staff to "Always wear the Thompson's smile." Next to it was a framed picture of the friendly butcher who fronted the current TV ads. He was a loveable Cockney, market trader-type who said things like 'Ave a butchers at our prices' or 'nothings fresher than our apples and pears'. I couldn't believe I was back, it felt like I'd been gone a year. The door opened and Dennis walked in.

"What happened to you? Fall out of bed?" he gestured towards my face with a grin.

"I got mugged."

"Oh dear, not your week is it? Oh well, you'd better come in," gesturing me into his office. He took his place behind his desk while I sat in one of the two vacant seats opposite. A framed photo of his wife and son stood on his desk and hung behind him was a picture of the store taken from the air by helicopter. Beside it was a picture of Dennis shaking hands with Mr Blobby. They met when he was drafted in to open the new Bristol Branch in 1993 after a double-booking meant two of the Gladiators couldn't make it.

"I'll get straight to the point," he said. "There's good news and there's bad news."

"Ok."

"This has been a bad week for everyone. Me, the store, Head Office-"

"Elaine Baker," I added.

"Yes of course Elaine Baker, but I meant everyone at Thompson's. This has been a bad week for us. An incident like this hits us hard. It hits us all hard. The public are bloody fickle, they vote with their feet. The opposition have been lapping it up. I ran into Malcolm Ellery the other day, my opposite number at Buy-Co. He said they've been rushed off their feet." I gave a concerned nod. "And Head Office have been going berserk. I've had Anthony Warren on the phone shitting bricks. The press have been all over us as well, we've been on damage limitation all week. They were talking about an eight per cent fall in share prices if she croaked it. It's been bad. It's been a bloody PR disaster. Darren Green was on the phone first thing Tuesday morning, his lot were worried. We've had people from London up here all week trying to sort it out. Health Inspectors sniffing around checking every department. The bloody unions have been involved. Steve Thompson demanded hour-by-hour updates to his villa in the Seychelles. His father's probably been doing somersaults in his grave. They were even talking about delaying the opening of four new stores because of all the bad publicity. I can honestly say I've never seen anything like it in 25 years of management. Pete Crosby said the same. He was brought in to head-up the internal investigation. He was supposed to be overseeing the new Thomo's DIY in Macclesfield this week but he's been down here fire fighting. We all have. Have you been on the floor?" he asked.

"No, I came straight up here."

"Bloody good job for your sake. There'd have lynched you. It's been a nightmare. They were all convinced the council were going to close us down and they'd be laid-off six-weeks before Christmas. I had Mary Bryant from HR up here in tears because of all the rumours. Barry Richmond and Jock McCall were threatening strike action if we closed; they even had a bloody website. I'll tell you straight Martin, your name has been mud around here, and not just at this branch. I had Rob Dale saying his lot in Cannock were fearing the worst as well. A memo's already gone out group-wide spelling out how things are going to have to change pronto because of this whole debacle. People aren't happy Martin. The whole of the OC staff are undergoing new training because of this. Us first, then nationwide by next Tuesday. They've drawn up a whole new seminar on it, called 'Food hygiene, it's for life'".

I nodded. He took a sip of coffee.

"We're a bloody laughing stock. I'm a laughing stock; I've seen internal emails calling for my head. They're now being investigated. Thankfully, London said from the word go that they were 110 per cent behind me but if it wasn't for 20 years dedication to this company things could have been very different." He sighed and shook his head. There was a moment of silence.

"So, how is Elaine Baker?" I asked. He frowned at me as if confused by the question.

"Well, she's out of ICU at least but it's still touch and go. The good news though is that her tests came back last night and they are saying it's impossible to say exactly when she contracted the virus. So far there's been no trace of salmonella in any of our departments meaning there's absolutely nothing concrete linking her to Thompson's in any way. I had to have a meeting with the lawyers who explained it all last night and we're watertight. It doesn't mean she didn't get it from us, just that there's no scientific proof that she did." Even for him that was a new low. "And the $64,000 question you want to ask is where does all this leave you?"

I held his gaze for a second before looking at the desk. "London were saying that the media would expect nothing short of a dismissal. Even Pete Crosby was saying you'd have to go. In short I had to fight tooth and bloody nail to keep you out the dole queue. I'm not gonna fire you Martin, but you came within a whisper of it. Head Office said ultimately the decision was mine to make and it was a tough one, I'll tell you that. But after giving it enormous consideration I'm throwing you a life-line. If this ship had gone down then we'd all have gone down with it. But she stayed afloat and I want you back on-board. That's the good news. The bad news is I've had to make some changes. Some have been handed down to me, others I was forced to make in your absence. After you left us up the creak without a paddle, it was all hands to the pump and I asked Carl to step into the breach. For the last five days he's been single-handedly running Produce and the OC, and in a word he's kept the whole bloody place from going under. And it's not gone unnoticed; he's earned some major Brownie points with Head Office. Pete Crosby's even talking about him taking on the new Peterborough branch when it opens in 2007. In the meantime though I'm promoting him into a new position I've created in charge of both the OC and Produce. You'll stay on as supervisor but you'll answer directly to Carl. Tony Fairfax has been made your opposite number on Produce. The new department will be operational immediately and Carl will be the head of OCP when he returns from the three-day break I've given him. Your position will hardly be affected, apart from the reduced responsibility, but it does mean I've had to freeze supervisors' yearly pay for the next three years and OCP staffing levels will be cut by around 15 per cent early in the New Year, to accommodate the increased managerial costs of the new department. Any questions?"

I didn't know where to start. Carl, that officious little sod, was going to be my boss? I hadn't been sacked but in the world of supermarket lower middle management there were far worse fates.

"Well what do you think? Head Office are actually quite impressed. I can see it going nationwide with us being used as a pilot and if it takes off it could be rolled out group-wide."

I paused for a moment weighing up what to say.

"Of course there is another choice," he said. "You don't have to stay. After everything that's happened nobody would be surprised if you waved the white flag and resigned. If there's one thing I've learned in 25 years of management it's not to focus on the problem but to look at the options. I'm not saying you should resign Martin, I'm just giving you options."

I looked up and decided I'd give it to him straight.

"Dennis, I just wondered how long your affair lasted with Jill from Accounts?"

"What?" His mouth actually fell open.

"You know, your affair? I hardly knew her, she left soon after I joined. Bit too much make-up for me, but she seemed nice. How did you get it on? Was it a conference or a Christmas party? Those things are a breeding ground for office romances."

His face grew a deeper red than I thought it was possible to go. It was an amazing moment.

"How dare you? You're sacked. On the spot. Have you forgotten who I am? I won't be spoken to like that. Who the hell do you think you are?" His phone beeped twice.

"You should check your mobile," I told him.

"You little shit, I want you off the premises immediately," he shouted.

"Just check your mobile,"

"I'm calling security," he blasted, reaching for the phone.

"The Stolen Kiss Wine Bar, Saturday November 9th 1985.

You were wearing a dark blue suit; she had on a fetching little white number with red stripes."

He opened his mouth to speak.

"Just check your mobile," I said. "Go on, for old time's sake."

He stood up slightly and pulled his phone free from his trouser pocket. He opened the handset and pressed the button with his stubby thumb. As the colour drained from his face I sent him another picture message, again from outside the wine bar but this time a close-up so that he and Jill filled the frame. The last picture was my favourite. I'd just ducked inside for a moment and from behind a mock-Roman pillar I'd snapped them from less than 10 feet away. Even in the candlelight it was perfectly clear who they were. He was almost looking straight at the camera, she was laughing. His right hand was in mid-air; his left hand was holding hers. His watch was visible and so was his lack of a wedding ring.

"How?" he asked. He looked broken.

"You both look very happy together," I said. "I wonder where you told your wife you were that night. Just doing something from the office?"

"How did you get this?" He looked at the screen in absolute shock.

"I remember that speech you gave at the last Christmas party, when you got your long service award, you said your wife had stood beside you for 26 years. Funny, I don't see her in any of those pictures."

"How dare you. What is this? What do you want?" He

217

growled as his shock gave over to anger.

"I want to leave Thompson's."

"Then go, I've just sacked you."

I shook my head, "No. I want to be made redundant."

"I can't."

"You already have."

"I can't. Even if I wanted to you can't just make people redundant, only their positions, it's the law."

"Then make mine redundant, do away with the supervisor role on the Oven Counter and I'll go and you'll never have to see me or my pictures again."

"I can't," he continued to argue. "Head Office would never allow the OC to run without a supervisor."

"But it's not the OC is it? It's OCP and it has a newly appointed manager to run it." This had worked out better than I'd expected.

"There's way too much work for just Carl, he'd be flat out."

"Dennis. DJ. I want full redundancy. I want a month and a half's salary for every one of the last 14 years I've worked here, I want my remaining 18 days holiday paid-out in full and I want Susan to ring me a taxi to the station."

"Or what? I suppose you'll show these to my wife?"

"No. Jill's husband. I only knew him by reputation. Big bloke I gather. Something to do with Welsh rugby, wasn't he?"

I got up to leave.

"Oh and one last thing," I added. "Steven Barns on the Oven Counter, I want you to up him to nine pound an hour, he's just become a father."

218

He looked again at the photos in disbelief.

"This is blackmail. I'll call the police."

"No, don't think of it as blackmail," I said as I walked towards the door. "Think of it as me giving you options."

My Nan was just falling asleep by the time I got to the ward
and I stayed in the corridor so as not to disturb her. The
doctors were pleased with the treatment so far but it would
take a lot more visits to the hospital in the coming months,
for her and for me. The anniversary was lovely and it
surprised me how happy Mom looked. She read a line from a
letter Dad had sent her while he was away with work. I had
just turned two and he said how pleased he'd been to have
the whole family over for my birthday. He ended by saying
how proud he was of his young family and how much he
missed us all when he was away. I'd never seen the letter
before and was amazed my Mom had kept it all those years.
She said that when she read it she could hear his words, like
he was talking to her. Talking to her from across time, I
thought. She was really pleased with the grave and although
she was sorry she had let it get in such a mess, she said there
were lots of other places that she remembered my Dad.
Dave and I spoke before the service, he'd heard about work
and asked if I was ok. He looks more and more like Dad
each time I see him. I apologised to Linda for the phone call
the other day and told her I didn't mean to upset her, she
said it was just a bad time, with the anniversary and all that.
Standing by the graveside, Mom said she and Dad were
talking about taking us abroad for the first time the following
year and that they were going to start saving after Christmas.
My Aunt Carol joked about the poor bloke my Dad was

supposed to be meeting that morning and how he must have been cursing him for being late. We all laughed and Mom explained that there was some truth in it as he was in a rush as he'd lost his keys the night before and spent ages searching the house for the spare. In the end it turned out that he'd dropped them in the garden and the paperboy must have found them as they were posted through the front door. He'd found them in the porch under a copy of the Daily Mail. I cried a lot that day. It was as if I'd finally tapped into my grief, and after opening the flood gates, I could start to let it out. Weeks later it dawned upon me that the whole time I was in the cemetery I didn't think once about 'the opening', I think I was too caught up in the present to worry about the past.

"Drunken Duck," said Craig excitedly.

"What?"

"Drunken Duck. He came home almost a length ahead to take Chepstow this afternoon."

"Your horse? Your three-legged no-hoper actually won?"

"Yep." And he handed me 200 quid. "And here's a little return on your investment."

"Thanks mate. How much did you win?"

"Two thousand seven hundred. Collected it this morning. I'm gonna surprise Linda and the kids, you know, now the anniversary's out the way."

"What are you gonna do?"

"Gonna take then to Florida, spend Christmas at Disneyland."

"Excellent. I'm really pleased for you."

"See, ye of little faith."

"Yep. And are you going to quit while you're ahead?"

"No chance, this is just the start of my run of luck. I put 150 quid on England winning the World Cup next year. They're gonna do it this time I just know it."

I'd just put some money in the coffee machine when Rachel appeared.

"Great minds think alike," she said. She was wearing lip-gloss and her hair was tied back in a high ponytail. She looked tired but beautiful.

"Here," I said. "Have this. I'm just down here to keep out of the way for a bit."

"Yeah, your sister said I might find you here."

"Are you on your break or do you have to rush back?"

"No, I've got a minute."

"Good, I just wanted to say sorry about the other night. I was acting strange and...." I wasn't really sure how to explain it.

She nodded.

"You were a bit. Your cousin, Danny was it? He said you weren't yourself. That you've had some problems at work."

"Yeah, sort of."

"Is it to do with that bloke I saw the other day? He was a right little jobsworth?"

"Partly but it's all ok now. I've got a new job."

"Where?"

"Do you know Andy's Videos in Erdington? I start on

Monday."

"Great. You really didn't suit the hats at Thompson's. Although I won't be able to come and visit you for chicken nuggets now."

"I'm sure I can do you a discount on DVDs."

"I haven't got one. Still got an old fashioned video. I don't really get time to watch that many films."

"You realise that's actually blasphemy to a video store clerk, don't you."

She laughed.

"When was the last time you went to the cinema?"

"Ages. Years probably."

"That's it then, I cordially invite you to the Odeon tonight, my shout. Popcorn and a drink included."

She thought about it for a second.

"I'd love to, I really would but my Mom's away on one of her Rotary trips so there's no one to look after Joe."

"Bring him along," I told her, I wasn't falling at the final hurdle.

"I don't know, he's a bit...."

"He'll be fine, he can choose. I'll pay. You just have to look embarrassed when I tell him what you were like at school." She smiled.

"Ok then I'll-" Her pager went off. "Gotta run. Sorry. My number's in the book, call me." She handed me the coffee and raced out of the door. I looked down at the paper cup, there was a smudge of lip gloss on one side. My thoughts turned to tonight, what should we see? What would Joe want to see? I was his age when Dave and his mates snuck me in to see Lethal Weapon, it was my first 18 rated film, my hair slicked-back to look older and my fake date of birth memorised just in case I was asked. I couldn't wait to grow up then and see what I wanted to at the pictures. I used to wish away the years to make it happen. A lot's changed since then, I don't tend to worry about the future too much these days, it comes around soon enough.

Epilogue
Monday July 11th 2011

It's been almost six years since the events of November 2005 and although the memories are fading, the effects of that time are as evident in my life as ever.

Elaine Baker made a full recovery. She spent three weeks in hospital where she steadily responded to the treatment, before being allowed home for Christmas. I read in the papers the following year that she received a 'six-figure out-of-court settlement' from ARG Foods, one of Thompson's main suppliers, after 'bacteria consistent with the salmonella germ' was identified in one of its poultry farms.

Six months later, when it felt like the dust had settled, I spent the day at Birmingham Central Library to research my 80s encounter with the police, under the pretext of investigating my family tree. Once in front of the Microfiche with the relevant year magnified onto the screen I scanned through copies of the Sutton Coldfield Observer and the Birmingham Mail for reports of my arrest. The day after my escape the Mail ran a witness appeal on page two asking for information about a man fitting my description. The following week the Observer printed details of Shaun Byford's arrest in relation to a missing woman. He was held for seven hours before being released without charge. Other than that there was nothing. Expanding my search into the local history section I found a copy of Birmingham Myths,

Mysteries & Ghost Stories, published in 1998. It included five late-night 'sightings' of a ghostly figure in St John's graveyard, said to be that of a murdered woman called 'Jilted Jenny', who was killed by her angry fiancé and buried in one of the graves.

Thinking back to that night, it was dark, the weather was bad and people don't just disappear - even when you've seen them disappear. I guess someone said they saw me make a dash for the fence and that became the official version. It was impossible for me to know without running the risk of attracting attention, particularly as they would have had my fingerprints on file, so it was best to leave it to speculation. One thing I did notice while scouring the local archives was an obituary for 'Local Lawyer' Malcolm Barrowclough who died of a heart attack the morning I left. I looked at the picture of him in his office at Barrowclough and Barlow Solicitors and thought about how hard he'd fought to get me to the graveyard. He'd been rushed to St Mary's Hospital after working as the Duty Solicitor on an 'important' but non-specified case. A quote from his partner William Barlow said he'd 'fought for justice for over 30 years' and I felt glad to have been his last client, I only wish I had tried harder to persuade him to go to the hospital.

Rachel and I were married on August 11th 2006 and although Joe's initial reaction to me was at best defiant, it was helped when we began renting PlayStation 3 games at the shop. These days, he comes back from university a few times a term and we usually go to the football. He's studying medicine and although I'm never specific I try to impress upon him that there are a great many discoveries still to be made.

My Nan survived for more than six months after her treatment but passed away in the summer of 2006. Even at the time the sadness I felt was secondary to the thought of her dancing to Elvis again in my Grandad's arms. Dave comes up to visit every now and then and we have a laugh as he reminds me of the things I'd forgotten about our childhood. Linda and Craig had another daughter two years ago and my Mom loves babysitting for them all. I'm glad Mom has Linda, they really need each other.

Andy and I opened our second branch in 2007 with the last of my redundancy money. We have a small team of bright, dedicated film-loving employees but have resisted the introduction of matching uniforms, motivational posters or a mission statement.

I go to the cemetery once a week to speak to my Dad and to keep the weeds back. I've thought a lot about 'the opening' and why a strange portal back in time would exist in a Birmingham cemetery. I've tried to make sense of quantum theory, of wormholes and any other possible explanations. Years later I found *Le Voyageur Imprudent* (The Unwary Traveller) written by René Barjavel in 1943. In it he describes how it would be impossible to travel back in time and kill your own Grandfather, because in doing so you would never be born and therefore never travelled back in time to kill him. It made a lot of sense. Another theory, the 'Novikov self-consistency principle', says that anything a would-be time traveller tried to do would be useless as their actions were already part of the history that had taken place. I've thought about *my* actions that week, the changes I could have made and the outcomes that stayed the same. I'd changed nothing. You can't go back and kill your grandfather as a younger man, just like you can't prevent your father from being killed. That was the unwritten rule to stop us messing around with things we shouldn't. But if I could make an addition to Novikov's principal, it would be that - just because I couldn't save my Dad, doesn't mean I couldn't get to know him a little better. In the years since, I've stood beside 'the opening' hundreds of times but I've never gone back through, I guess I'm too occupied with the present to worry about going back to the past.

Printed in Great Britain
by Amazon

30500604R00137